L5:
Behind the
MOON

By Steve Tracy

Property of Hartman
Middle School

Silver Burdett Press
Parsippany, New Jersey

This one is for Erin Tormey.
Without her talent, imagination, story-telling,
and love, it would have been impossible.

Text © 1995 by Steve Tracy
Cover Illustration © 1995 by Tom Curry

Published by Silver Burdett Press,
A Simon & Schuster Company
299 Jefferson Road, Parsippany, New Jersey 07054

Designed by JP Design Associates

Manufactured in Mexico

10 9 8 7 6 5 4 3 2 1

Library of Congress Cataloging-in-Publication Data
Tracy, Steve.
L5: behind the moon/by Steve Tracy. p. cm.
Summary: Amelia, a young Earth girl in a wheelchair,
joins her father at a colony behind the moon and
becomes embroiled in a life-threatening mystery.
[1. Physically handicapped—Fiction. 2. Wheelchairs—
Fiction. 3. Mystery and detective stories. 4. Science
fiction.] I. Title.
PZ7.T6834Lab 1995
[Fic]—dc20 94-39397 CIP AC
ISBN 0-382-24761-2 (LSB)   ISBN 0-382-24708-6 (SC)

It is the year 2060. People now live in space. A huge space station follows the moon in its orbit. There is a smaller colony of settlers on the moon itself.

There are five points in space called Lagrange points, where the gravity of the moon and the earth balance each other. An object at one of these points, no matter how large, tends to stay there, rather than falling toward either the moon or Earth. Two of these points are especially stable and are called L4 and L5. Both are located in the moon's orbit, but L4 lies ahead of the moon and L5 behind the moon. Both points are 240,000 miles from the moon, which is also the approximate distance of the earth from the moon.

In the year 2015, pioneers from Earth built a space station at L5. The inhabitants of the L5 Colony proudly wear a triangular badge. It symbolizes the triangle formed by the earth, the L5 point, and the moon. Colonists on the moon, however, do not wear the triangle.

People have brought some differences with them into outer space. Several generations of people living in quite different environments have produced other differences. In addition, relations between the settlers on the moon and the Space Station have been strained by some strange recent events. Some L-Fivers blame the lunar settlers. Tensions between the L5 colonists and the lunar settlers are gradually increasing and are nearing the flash point.

No one has yet considered that something alive, something with purposes of its own, is seeking to survive and grow.

Amelia revved up her wheelchair and lowered the treads so that it had the traction of a small bulldozer. Off the wooden boardwalk, she needed all its power to travel over the sand toward the bare rocks. She was hot in her wet suit, but she wanted to dive one last time.

It was low tide and the beach sand was firm. The moon hung like a faded disk in the morning sky, pale, almost transparent. But it was the moon that moved the ocean's tides. That thin silver disk pulled at the blue Pacific with a force twice as strong as the sun, exposing a crescent of damp, white sand and rocky tide pools.

Amelia aimed her wheelchair over the sand, to the edge of the lacy waves.

She followed a shoal of sand into the tide pools— ordinarily under several feet of water—now exposed. She brushed her rust-colored hair back from her cheeks. She looked up at the moon. That was where her father was. And that is where she would be tomorrow.

In the meantime, she wanted to see the tide pools one last time. Her wheelchair hummed softly as it laid down its track among the skittery star tracks of sanderlings and sandpipers. She maneuvered it into position at the edge of a long, quiet pool, motionless except for the gentle flux of water moving in and out like a breeze. Seaweed—eelgrass, winged kelp, feather boa, surf grass, and sea palms—swayed first this way, then that, at certain angles glistening like an oil slick.

Sea anemones opened like huge green and pink flowers, waving their tentacles. The longer she watched, the more she saw. She saw tiny crabs scuttling sideways along the crevices. She saw speckled fish called sculpin, blending with the rocks so that they were visible only when they moved.

Then Amelia saw something she had never seen before. A hermit crab maneuvered itself up against a purple turban shell. Amelia knew that hermit crabs don't have their own shells. They borrow shells as they grow, changing them as needed. They need a shell to protect their large, tender abdomens, sealing off the opening with their two claws once they're inside. The crab Amelia was watching suddenly scooted out of its old shell and backed its behind quickly into the new home.

This comforted Amelia. She wasn't the only one leaving home. Still, the hermit crab probably wouldn't miss anyone the way Amelia was already missing her grandparents. And the hermit crab didn't have to travel 240,000 miles to arrive at its new home, leaving behind all that was familiar.

Since the accident two years ago, Amelia had lived with her grandparents in Pacific Grove, a little town in California. Her father had come back from the Space Station for her mother's funeral, but she hadn't seen him since then. In fact, she hadn't seen much of him for the last five years. Now he wanted her to join him. She wondered why he had decided that now was the time.

Why did she have to leave two people she loved—Gramps and Grandma? Why did she have to leave Earth's comforting gravity for a spinning wheel in space? There was something going on with her father, but she didn't know exactly what it was. She just knew that she had to go. This would be her last day on Earth, at least for a while.

She looked up from the tide pool to see the moon, hanging like a faded, sun-bleached sand dollar in the sky. It was hard for Amelia to imagine that soon she would be part of a colony—along with about 200,000 other pioneers—drifting in orbit behind the moon.

She backed up her chair, swiveled it, and headed down the beach. A Siberian husky ran up to the chair and barked. Its owner called from a distance. Amelia smiled and scratched the dog's ears. It must be strange for a dog to see a wheelchair here on the beach. But she preferred the dog's puzzled barking to the stiff politeness she got from most people.

She herded a flock of sanderlings along the surf line. She came upon hundreds of tiny blue transparent jellyfish, washed up on the beach. The biggest were only four inches long, with tiny sails. They looked as if they were made of plastic, of cellophane. They had the wonderful scientific name *Velella velella,* and Amelia knew that they led strange lives. They began deep in the ocean, at about 7,000 feet, and gradually formed gas pockets that floated them to the surface. They had triangular sails and drifted with the wind. Some of them floated east and some of them west, depending on the angle of their sails. They had tiny stinging tentacles but were harmless, except to plankton, which they ate as they floated on the surface of the sea.

Amelia's mother, who had been a marine biologist, had taught her all of this. After the accident, her mother's ashes had been scattered here from the research boat where she had worked. So, in a way, this last visit to the tide pools and the beach was Amelia's last visit to her mother's grave. Although there was no marker, Amelia imagined a brass plate embedded in the barnacle-encrusted rock: Margaret Martine Mann 2020–2058.

The waves rolled in and rattled the pebbles. Amelia turned her wheelchair toward the surf and headed in. She clicked in the oxygen tanks and took the mouthpiece between her teeth. She pulled the mask over her face and wheeled into the sea. The cold water closed over her head. And she continued. She knew she shouldn't dive without a buddy, but she felt safe. She would ignore the rules just this once since she knew these waters so well. Beyond the surf line, visibility was good, about 80 feet. The wheelchair took her along the sandy bottom into water about 30 feet deep. Here, she was below the pull of ebb and flow. She unstrapped herself, took the tank on her back, and floated up from her wheelchair. She was free.

She swam along the rocks and through the kelp. She delighted in the rockfish. She noted the eels hidden in the crevices, peering out with their ugly, toothy grins. A sea otter dived and watched her for a moment. Who was this strange creature in the watery midst? She saw a pelican dive after a fish in a flurry of bubbles. Her own bubbles attracted curious fish, glinting in and out of the shafted sunlight. She would miss all this.

Finally, she swam back to the wheelchair, strapped herself in, and wheeled back to the surface, out of the gentle surf and onto the sand. She slipped her mask off her face. She took out her mouthpiece, turned off the air, and unstrapped her tanks. She was surprised to find herself crying. A person can't really control tears, no matter how hard he or she tries. They came, like the salty ocean, like tides pulled by the moon.

Warming in the sun, Amelia rolled across the sand to the wooden boardwalk, pulled up the tread, and traveled the two blocks back to her grandparents' house. Pink flowering ice plants bordered the path along the shore.

At her grandparents' home, Amelia had her own room, where she was surrounded by her own stuff and shelves of books. Her music stand stood in the middle of the room, and her violin case was open on the desk. (She found she practiced more if she always left the case open.) Her grandmother had been a librarian before most books were put on computers and before libraries had become banks of computers. Living in her grandparents' home was a little like living in a huge antique store.

Tonight would be a kind of special treat. For her last dinner on Earth, Amelia was able to choose any meal she wanted. Ordinarily, Amelia ate only vegetables, but tonight she wanted squid, fried lightly in batter, and served with a slice of lemon.

Somehow, squid were connected to her life. Gramps loved to tell the story of his own father, who didn't like squid but who wrote a cookbook of 201 squid recipes. He tested them out on his kids.

"Oh, Lord," Gramps had chuckled. "We had to eat them with tomato sauce. And as steaks. We had them in squid salads with vinegar. We dipped the tentacles in melted cheese. It was like one big science experiment, with my father observing, never tasting. He just wrote it all down, watching our faces."

Squid also reminded Amelia of her mother. One night, when Amelia had first gotten her scuba license, she was out on the research boat with her mother. Her mother took Amelia on her first night swim. They put on their wet suits, fins, weight belts, tanks, masks, and snorkels and climbed down the ladder into the black water.

They wore lights on their foreheads, like old-fashioned coal miners. But the light was swallowed up in the dark, dark water. There had been a full moon that night. It turned the surface of the ocean silver, like aluminum foil, all crinkly and bright. From twenty feet underwater, in a forest of kelp, their bubbles wobbled to the surface. The only notion of up and down came from the upward flight of the bubbles. Everything else was pitch black.

Then suddenly, a silvery presence moved around her all at once, and she thought, "Shark!" Then she realized that she was in the middle of a school of squid, all about eight inches long, sparkling blue and orange and silver, moving in one huge group. Her mother circled back through the kelp stalks and took her hand. This was something special.

"They were attracted by our light like moths," Amelia's mother explained when they were back on board. "That's how squid fishermen catch them. By shining bright lights on the water and circling the squid with nets. They catch them when they come in to breed."

That night they talked a little about Amelia's father. "I know it's hard for him to be gone so much," her mother had said. "I think we'll see him soon. I may have permanent work on the moon, helping out with a plankton project."

But the accident had put an end to their plans to join Amelia's father.

So now, in memory of her mother, of that last dive together, Amelia munched squid by candlelight. And a spinach salad from Gran's garden. Gramps had made a pie from the berries he grew in the back yard. Sometimes for special occasions, Gramps would go to the trouble of making homemade vanilla ice cream. He had done that tonight.

"Well, here's to our little girl," Gramps said, raising a glass of champagne. "Off to the moon." Gramps had long, white hair and a full beard. "Who would a thunk it, when I was born in 1969, that I would see a granddaughter go to live on the Space Station? Who would have thought that I would live to be 91 years old?"

"Especially with those cigars," Gran said. "You should have died young."

"Only the good die young," Gramps quipped. He only smoked cigars in the garden and in his cottage behind the main house. He and Gran had been arguing about this nasty habit for half a century.

"This is very good squid," Gramps said, tactfully changing the subject.

A cat curled in his lap. He was a comfortable man. He had worked as a horseshoer, a journalist, a writer, a teacher, a dishwasher, and a bartender.

For the last five years, Gramps had been Amelia's substitute father. He had taught her how to garden. He had shown her the "three sisters," as the Indians called them—squash, corn, and beans. "They all grow together," he said. "The beans restore nutrients to the soil. The squash provide protection around the roots by shading them from the sun. Plus, raccoons don't like the leaves of squash, so they leave the corn alone. The corn provides a frame for the beans to grow on.

They all depend on each other."

When dinner was over, they gathered around the fire-place and watched the low flames flicker in the darkness. Gramps recited a poem. He loved poetry and knew a lot of it by heart. He tried to memorize ten lines a week. "It doesn't seem like a lot, but it's surprisingly difficult," he said. Amelia had tried but found herself cheating, using the words of pop songs instead. "Oh, I do that, too," Gramps said. "One week, I used the Pledge of Allegiance to fill the quota."

Tonight, Gramps chose "The Owl and the Pussy-Cat" by Edward Lear. His voice was like his hair—soft and silver. There always seemed to be a laugh bubbling up in it.

The Owl and the Pussy-Cat went to sea
In a beautiful pea-green boat:
They took some honey, and plenty of money
Wrapped up in a five-pound note.
The Owl looked up to the stars above,
And sang to a small guitar,
"O lovely Pussy, O Pussy, my love,
What a beautiful Pussy you are,
You are,
You are!
What a beautiful Pussy you are!

Pussy said to the Owl, "You elegant fowl,
How charmingly sweet you sing!

Oh! let us be married; too long we have tarried:
But what shall we do for a ring?"
They sailed away, for a year and a day,
To the land where the bong-tree grows;
And there in a wood a Piggy-wig stood,
With a ring at the end of his nose,
His nose,
His nose,
With a ring at the end of his nose.

Gramps paused, winked at Gran, and then gazed for a long moment into the fire, as though he had forgotten the rest. Then he smiled at Amelia, and looking into her eyes, he went on, with just a touch of sadness in his voice. Gramps knew that Amelia was leaving.

"Dear Pig, are you willing to sell for one shilling
Your ring?" Said the Piggy, "I will."
So they took it away, and were married next day
By the turkey who lives on the hill.
They dined on mince and slices of quince,
Which they ate with a runcible spoon;
And hand in hand, on the edge of the sand,
They danced by the light of the moon,
The moon,
The moon,
They danced by the light of the moon.

Early in the morning, Amelia's grandparents drove her to the Aerospace port and checked her in for the flight. Then they waited, sipping tea, and looking at the sharp-nosed plane that would carry Amelia to the Space Colony. Gramps explained that it was a hypersonic Scramjet—holding about 200 passengers. It used hydrogen fuel mixed with air and could fly 25 times the speed of sound once it got into space. He had actually flown to the Space Station once, as a newspaper reporter. "The best part is the weightlessness," he said. "That's the weirdest part. You'll like it, Amelia."

They had never really been separated before, so Amelia, Gran, and Gramps exchanged many good-bye kisses and hugs. Then Amelia was allowed to board. A few families with young children followed her. Then the rest of the 200 passengers boarded the Scramjet, all bound for the Space Station.

"Have you flown before?" the flight attendant asked her.

"Yes, once," Amelia said. But she didn't add that she had been a passenger in the infamous crash of the Scramjet two years ago. Amelia and her mother had had plans to join her father for his birthday and then spend a month with him. If they liked the Space Station, they might stay longer. The Scramjet had streaked down the runway and had collided with a maintenance vehicle. Then the Scramjet burst into flames— the hydrogen fuel exploding in a deafening blast. Amelia was grabbed by her mother and practically thrown out of the cabin, high above the wreckage-strewn runway. She remembered rolling out of the flaming cabin, amid screams and smoke. She was one of the few lucky survivors, but her spine had been damaged in a way that doctors could not yet repair. Her mother had died, just a little behind but a little too late.

Now, two years later, the plane taxied out to the runway, fired up, and rose quickly and smoothly. In seconds, it was out over San Francisco Bay and the coast of California. The ship began to vibrate as the rocket boosters kicked in and built up more and more thrust.

The noise and vibration increased.

Amelia didn't know how she would feel when she heard the engines fire up. She expected to be terrified, but she wasn't. Amelia was pleasantly surprised because the very beginnings of things were important. Her violin teacher had always said, "Get the beginning and ending right. The audience will forget the rest. In fact, they might just sleep through it."

As the ship gained speed, Amelia felt herself pushed back against the seat, which was designed to cushion about three times Earth's normal gravity. About 30 seconds into the flight, the blue sky of Earth turned jet black, blacker than the night sky. About 28 miles above Earth, the ship was out of the atmosphere. And there was no air here to reflect the sunlight. Within minutes, the plane was cruising at five times the speed of sound. It would only take two hours to fly to Tokyo, but the trip to the Space Colony would take about ten hours.

She would have plenty of time to read or listen to the information on the Space Colony. For now, she ate a breakfast of bran flakes, a breakfast roll, peach yogurt, and tea. With all the changes that were about to occur, the tea she cupped in her hands provided warm comfort.

Then Amelia got her first glimpse of Earth. Of course, she had seen pictures. But there it was—hanging like a blue pearl in black velvet. Clouds swirled over the surface. Her grandmother and grandfather were there, probably in their little house in Pacific Grove by now. Everything was on that little ball.

All of life, all of human history, came out of that ball. It all seemed so fragile, like a tide pool.

It was the water that made Earth so beautiful and blue. Her mother had always smelled of sea water since she spent her days diving and working on the boat or in the lab, which was filled with giant saltwater tanks that held crabs, and octopus, starfish, and sea urchins. Amelia closed her eyes.

About midway through the flight, Amelia plugged in the video about the Space Station. Her father had been a commander there for the last five years, but she thought it would be a good idea to refresh her memory. She watched it on a small screen on the back of the seat in front of her, listening to the audio on headphones.

According to the video, the Space Station had been built by pioneers from Earth in the year 2015—forty-five years ago. It resembled a giant wheel about five miles in diameter. As it followed the moon in its orbit, the station rotated. The spinning created centripetal force—like a whirling carnival ride. At the outside rim of the wheel, this force resulted in an artificial gravity. As a result, people who lived and worked in that area felt much as they would have on Earth. Altogether, about 200,000 people inhabited the Space Station. Some of them had been born there and had never even been to Earth.

Most of the materials used to construct the Space Station—like iron and nickel and titanium—along with its water and oxygen, came from the Lunar Colony. A machine called a mass driver slung chunks of ore in a continuous stream from the surface of the moon. These chunks were collected in an orbiting factory. There they were shaped into products that were then taken to Earth or the Space Station.

The energy to run the Space Station was provided mostly by huge solar collectors, which also beamed energy back to Earth in the form of microwaves, to be converted into electricity. The video also described a new project on the lunar surface. Using the "stardust" that had collected for billions of years as fuel, the lunar colonists were building a fusion reactor—a reactor that mimicked the process that powers all stars, including the sun. This stardust, called helium 3, would provide vast amounts of energy.

Amelia listened to a long, boring section about space treaties. One phrase stuck with her. "The Moon and other celestial bodies shall be the province of all humankind." No Earth nation or bloc had the right to own or control the moon or asteroids, or space itself, she thought. The Space Settlement Law of 2010, an international treaty, had made law of all this. It struck Amelia that a lot of space treaties were based on the law of the sea, which in all human history no nation was foolish enough to claim. Outer space, like the ocean, seemed to make people sensible.

The video ended with the suggestion that a new kind of human was evolving. These humans would be uniquely adapted to life in space. Having adjusted to living in reduced gravity, they might actually be unable to live on Earth. Basically these humans would be ready to proceed into the broader reaches of space. Mars was the next step.

Amelia removed the headphones. That was enough science for a while. She was beginning to feel a little overloaded. And she really didn't like being fed information. She would learn more about the Space Station once she was there. She wondered how playing the violin would feel in zero gravity.

3

CHAPTER

Amelia awoke to a view of the silver wheel, spinning and gleaming in the sunlight, and the tug of engines slowing the Scramjet. As the ship glided quietly to the hub of the wheel, Amelia realized how huge the Space Station was. As she looked from the hub, the rim of the wheel filled the horizon like a wreath of huge sausages.

The Scramjet clicked to a stop. Amelia drifted slightly in her seat, weightless. Other passengers were also experimenting with this strange new state. She undid her seat belt and for the first time in two years, except for scuba diving, she was free of the weight of her legs.

"You can ride in your wheelchair if you want," a flight attendant said, "but we'll have to put an electromagnet on it to hold it right side up and give you traction. Or you can simply lock onto the exit ramp. It's like a conveyor belt. Just hang onto the straps. You won't really need your chair until you get to the rim."

"Please fold it," Amelia said. And she was maneuvered effortlessly onto the exit ramp, floating like seaweed. Amelia left the ship for the docking port.

Here, at the center of the hub, the wheel's centripetal force didn't supply the artificial gravity that colonists felt throughout most of the Space Station. Everywhere around Amelia, the new arrivals giggled and laughed at the feeling of not weighing anything. Some of them would stay in the Nippon Space Hotel. There they could play a form of golf where a drive or a putt could go for several miles. Space golf had become quite popular.

For Amelia, weightlessness went beyond golf or laughter. Now she could move as freely as anyone else, and in some ways she even had an advantage. In a weightless state, most people found their powerful leg muscles a real bother, because one kick could send a person stumbling about, almost always in the wrong direction. In a weightless environment, legs were useless, even a handicap.

A tall man with a red beard hovered at the end of the ramp as Amelia floated into the hub. He stood out in the crowd waiting to meet the newcomers. He was dressed in a dark blue uniform with a triangle badge of pale blue. Amelia remembered that the triangle was the symbol of the lines between the earth and the moon and L5. They created an equilateral triangle.

Even floating weightless, almost without motion, the man had a certain weight and stern dignity to him. The name *Commander Mann* was embroidered above his triangle badge.

"Papa?" She wasn't entirely sure.

"Amelia," he said softly. And now she recognized her father, thinner and strangely taller than she remembered. And the beard was new. She had always called him "Papa," not Commander Mann. The faintest of smiles played over his lips, and he reached down to her to give her a stiff hug and a kiss on the cheek.

"Papa," she said, "I'm here."

"Yes, you are," he answered. "At long last. I have missed you so much."

Amelia began to say that she had missed him too, but stopped. In fact, she hadn't missed him. She had never really known him.

"I've thought about you a lot," she said instead.

She was a little uncomfortable under his long look. Was there a hint of sadness there? Why?

"Well, let me show you your new home," he said finally. "We have a little trip ahead of us."

"I'm getting used to trips," Amelia said, and her father smiled again. She noticed that his hands were freckled.

Together they boarded a coach, something like a subway, which traveled along the spoke from the hub of the Space Station toward the outer rim. "We call this the Whoosh," her father said.

He launched into an explanation of the Space Station's construction.

"The outer rim of this doughnut is made of glass and thick aluminum wrapped in cable for shielding against radiation," Amelia's father said quickly. "The glass we use, built right here from Moon rock, is heat-resistant and filters out harmful radiation. The heat and radiation can be dangerous, but that's where the Space Station gets a lot of its power—as well as beaming microwave energy back to Earth."

The Whoosh wheezed to a halt and the doors slipped open, revealing a gleaming hallway, washed in pale green light. "We're about halfway out the doughnut. These will be your quarters, at least for the time being," Amelia's father said, leading her out of the car and into the hallway. A man in uniform followed with Amelia's luggage, her violin, and her wheelchair.

Her father pushed back a folding door and showed Amelia her room. A sleeping bag was attached to the wall in a kind of cabinet. "Gravity is nil here," he said. "And people find they sleep better when they're attached to something. If you want, though, you can just float.

"This is your shower module. It'll take a little getting used to. Our gravity space is at a premium, so we live mostly in the zero-gravity zones.

"Water doesn't exactly flow down here. It tends to float around. And it can work its way into the electrical system, so showers are enclosed. You're allowed one shower every three days. Water is also precious here. You get sprayed and a vacuum sucks the water away to be recycled. There's a video orientation for all this," he said, flicking on a large screen. "All the information you'll need is available. Plus we get all the Earth stations and channels, and there's a complete CD-ROM library. You shouldn't be bored.

"And this is your communicator," he said, strapping a bracelet that looked like a wristwatch to Amelia's arm. "This allows you to talk almost instantly with Earth—with Gramps and Gran for example—as well as anyone in the Space Station. I've sent them both communicators. Of course, dialing Earth is a long distance call." Amelia looked for a grin but didn't find one.

"I'll introduce you to the Space Cadets—kids about your age. And I want to show you the 'countryside.' But I imagine you're a little tired after your trip and probably need to settle in."

"Papa," Amelia asked suddenly. "What do you do here?"

Her father shook his head. "Well, sometimes I wonder. That's complicated. Technically, I'm Environmental Systems Commander. In rank, I'm second in command. Right now, I'm busy mostly with our recycling efforts and dealing with 45 years of garbage. Commander Stewart is my boss. We'll have dinner with Commander Stewart this evening. And tomorrow, I'll show you around. I'll be back in a few minutes. I'm right next door. Eventually, we'll move to the gravity sector in the Farm Zone—if all goes as planned. In the meantime, just call me on the communicator if you need anything," he finished in a rush.

"I'm glad you're here," he added as he drifted away.

Amelia was left in her room, 240,000 miles from Earth. But she felt most distant from her wheelchair. She could float free now!

The video orientation played in full color. The tape explained that going to the bathroom in space was complicated. First, Amelia would have to anchor her feet under a bar and use the hand grips—just to hold herself in place. Then the vacuum system kicked in. All waste was recycled for its valuable nitrogen and liquids. Samples were chilled, vacuum-dried, and analyzed by lab robots. The health of all the Space Station pioneers was automatically monitored on a regular basis.

"That's gross," Amelia thought. She would have to get used to a lot of things.

She thought she'd try a shower first. She simply left her clothes floating around the cabin and climbed into what looked like a tall washing machine. There were no faucets, only buttons. She pushed one, and streams of warm water hit her from all sides. "This is like a car wash!" Amelia thought, but the shower felt awfully good. Just as her father said, the water formed little balls and floated around her. She pushed the other button, and the water was sucked from the chamber. Then hot air shot from other jets. "So much for needing a towel," she thought, emerging dry and warm.

What should she wear for her first day in space? She put on a pair of overalls.

For the first time, Amelia noticed a pair of delicate headphones clamped to one wall. A little sign said TAS. She punched up those three letters on the CD-ROM.

TAS stood for "Thought Amplification and Synchronization." By putting on the earphones and focusing your mind, you could throw your thoughts. These thoughts were amplified, processed by a central computer, and broadcast. In this way, everyone in the Space Station could communicate almost instantaneously on one large network. It was still in the experimental stages, and the Space Station was the laboratory. According to the video briefing, the program promoted cooperation and a sense of community. "We live in the emptiness of space, but none of us need to be alone. Linked together, we can help in emergencies and solve our problems in tranquility. Together we are smarter than any one of us is alone."

Amelia thought it sounded kind of crowded. She couldn't imagine wanting to share every thought, especially since she was basically shut up with these same two hundred thousand people in a spinning doughnut.

Well, she could try TAS later. She suddenly felt very, very tired. What she needed was a good nap.

The sleeping compartment was essentially a narrow, padded closet with straps to hold you in. She floated into it, wondering if she could sleep standing up, and dozed immediately. She dreamed of her grandparents' house in Pacific Grove and the ocean.

She woke up to the sound of someone knocking at her door. It was her father. She crawled out of the sleep station, like a butterfly emerging from a cocoon.

"How did you enjoy your first nap in space?" he asked.

"I dreamed of Earth," Amelia said. "And Gran and Gramps. And tide pools."

They floated together. "I have such dreams, too," her father said, smoothing her rumpled hair with his hand, "even after all these years."

They took the Whoosh out to the rim and emerged in a huge tube filled with trees and pasture. "This is the Farm Zone," Commander Mann explained as he settled Amelia in her wheelchair. "It's the largest of the modules, about the size of San Francisco. There are other modules dedicated to research and manufacturing. Most of our food comes from here. A few people actually live here."

Amelia was not thrilled that she again needed her wheelchair. She was even less pleased that her father was pushing her instead of letting her drive. But she didn't say anything. There were no large roads here, only neatly kept paths and people walking or riding horses. At last, they stopped at a large log cabin in a meadow, surrounded by pine trees, a garden, and an orchard of apple, plum, peach, and walnut trees. In the garden, Amelia noticed corn, squash, and beans—the old three Indian sisters Gramps had taught her about.

"This is Commander Stewart's home," her father said, as they approached the house. A tall, elegant, copper-skinned woman appeared in the doorway.

Commander Stewart strode toward them, flashed a wide smile, and said, "Welcome." For the first time, Amelia felt genuinely welcome, genuinely at home. Elizabeth had a powerful handshake, but then she hugged Amelia, and the hug was like a homecoming. Amelia found herself leaning into it and being lifted into warmth and security. It took her out of her wheelchair.

"Your father has told me much about you," Elizabeth said to Amelia.

Inside there was an enormous banquet hall. Its size astonished Amelia."I'm the commander, after all," Elizabeth said to Amelia, and winked. "I have to entertain. In a pinch, this hall will hold one half of one percent of the population."

The ceilings were almost twenty feet high, supported by thick redwood beams. Skylights let light in and allowed a view of both the earth and the moon overhead. But there was also a huge loom, with a rug in progress. Richly colored rugs hung on the walls like paintings. It was kind of like a great lodge, and it reminded Amelia of ancient paintings she had once seen. Amelia felt as if she had traveled back in time.

Elizabeth moved with certainty through the large space. Huge tables were set with white napkins and silver. "You're our guest of honor," Commander Stewart said. "I've invited a few people I'd like you to meet."

Shortly after, about two dozen kids arrived, all wearing TAS earphones. The boys and girls were American, African, European, and Asian-looking, but they all wore the same white uniform of baggy shirts and pants. Amelia assumed they were locked into TAS. "We're glad you're here," one of them, said. "I'm Lila. Our group is called the Space Cadets. We represent 20,000 of the Space Station's young people. We welcome new members. We invite you to join us."

"That would be nice," Amelia said. Lila was probably African and had a round, friendly face. But her voice was curiously flat, like a computer or a robot. Amelia wished that Lila would take off her earphones. They were just as distracting as mirrored sunglasses. Amelia talked to about a dozen of the Space Cadets. The all had that same flat, sweet voice and seemed to be listening with their eyes.

"We have several orientations, which would be good for you to catch," Lila said. "We have many activities. We have many games. All virtual reality, of course. PacPerson is my favorite. Favfav."

Other Space Cadets echoed Lila's words. "PacPerson. Favfav, favfav." Amelia figured out what *favfav* meant. "You will need clothes," Lila added. "Yours are sillywilly."

"Sillywilly, sillywilly," other Cadets repeated.

"How rude," Amelia thought, but didn't say so. She would keep her overalls.

Finally, the meal was served. Amelia loved it, in part

because she sat right next to Commander Stewart. There was lasagna made from wheat and spinach and tomatoes and cheese, all produced by the colonists of the Space Station. There were salads and fruits, which were also grown in the Farm Zone. There was—for the kids—a bubbly orange drink that truly was delicious.

After dinner, the lights were turned down and Elizabeth spoke. Everyone was relaxed in their chairs, sipping tea.

"Living in space makes us look back for roots," Elizabeth said. "As most of you know, I was raised on the moon, but my own roots go back to Earth, to California. Long ago," Elizabeth said, "our people told this story. My people were the Karok, Native Americans on Earth.

"As you all know," Elizabeth continued, her clear mellow voice filling the hall, "the moon has long been associated with female gods like the Roman moon goddess Diana. But among my people, the story goes, the Sun and the Moon were sister and brother. At first they refused to rise, staying in their house of solid stone. Many people visited the house to see if they could get the Sun and the Moon to rise, but all failed. They could not even enter the house build of solid stone. Finally, Earth Worm and Gopher, who carried a bag of fleas, decided to dig a tunnel under the stone walls. The tunnel came into the house, and Gopher opened his bag of fleas. The fleas began biting Sun and Moon and made their life miserable, so they decided to leave the stone house.

"We cannot travel together," Moon said to Sun. "Do you

wish to travel by day or night?"

"At first, Sun tried to travel by night, but all the Stars fell in love with her and kept her from traveling. Sun went back and told her brother Moon that he must go by night. This he agreed to and has done ever since."

Elizabeth continued the story, with a glance at Amelia's father. "Moon was disliked by everybody. Because of this he didn't care whom he chose for a wife, and so he married Rattlesnake, Grizzly Bear, and Frog.

"Many people visited Moon and tried to get rid of him. Lizard visited and started eating Moon. Just as he was nearly finished, Frog, one of Moon's wives, came upon Lizard and chased him away. Then, with some of Moon's blood, Frog made Moon over, until he was large again.

"Lizard is always returning and eating Moon, and each time Frog chases him away just in time and makes Moon over again. That is why, today, we sometimes see all of Moon, and then he gets smaller and smaller until he disappears from our sight.

"You can still see Frog in Moon if you look closely," Elizabeth said. "And Lizard."

"Nobody likes Moon, even today," Commander Mann muttered. Elizabeth glanced at him, concern and annoyance flickering in her eyes.

Amelia loved the storytelling. It reminded her of all the times that she and Gran and Gramps read to each other around the fire.

On the way home, her father asked Amelia what she thought of Elizabeth. "She reminds me of Mom," Amelia said. "I mean, she doesn't look anything like Mom."

"I had the same reaction," her father said.

"I could do without the Space Cadets," Amelia added. "They're strange."

"Be patient," her father advised. "They're not bad kids. You'll get used to them."

"Not sure I want to," Amelia murmured, a bit defiantly. Her father sighed, as though he had many burdens, and this was the least of them.

That night Amelia looked out to the moon and tried to see Frog there in the shadows.

"We'll take the MMU," Commander Mann said the next morning as he and Amelia took the Whoosh to the zero-gravity hub of the Colony.

"What's an MMU?" she asked.

"Moon Manned Unit," her father replied. "They're how we get around outside the Colony. We have about 50 of them. Not just anyone can check one out. But you can, because as my daughter you have some perks. The Space Cadets will be a bit jealous, I'm sure."

Amelia still delighted in the weightlessness. She would not need help from her wheelchair into the MMU.

Once inside the MMU, her father opened the docking port and fired the hydrogen rockets. They lifted out of the station into the vacuum of space. "Don't forget your TAS," her father said, just as Gran used to remind her to fasten her seatbelt. He slipped the phones on and Amelia followed his example.

She experienced a buzzy hum. At first, it seemed like static, but then she recognized the Space Cadets, on a kind of channel of their own. She could hear them chattering about the war games. She recognized her father's thoughts—closer, more vivid. He was talking to her without speaking, simply thinking to her. It was about the weirdest thing Amelia had ever felt.

She imagined that it took some practice to channel thoughts as clearly as her father did it, even though the computer filtered out a lot of the other mental activity. With practice, she knew, an experienced user could pick and choose which ideas would be transmitted. Her father TASed to her, "It goes without saying."

"Favfav," Amelia teased back but got nothing in return.

"First, we'll visit the SPS—the solar power station," her father said crisply, guiding the MMU into the blackness. That system was a huge network of grids and solar cells. "It's over 3,000 feet across and it was built here," her father said. "It weighs about 50,000 tons. On Earth, the atmosphere filters out most of the sun's energy. You get only one billionth of the energy. In space, you get it full force, and it can produce enough energy for not only the Colony but Earth as well. Most of the materials for the SPS came from the moon."

Next, her father adjusted the thrusters, and the MMU traveled close to one of the satellites responsible for the communication with Earth. "That's what our communicators are networked to. And TAS uses the same system. Those satellites are what make it all possible. They transmit the equivalent of a 20-volume encyclopedia every second."

Her father also showed her the space telescope. He said it was six miles across and had its own rocket engines. "Out here, without an atmosphere, the stars don't twinkle," he explained. "Using this telescope, astronomers can see things fifty times fainter than anything visible from Earth. We could see the face on a dime from 372 miles away!"

Amelia thought that was fairly interesting, although she had no particular interest in looking at a dime from that distance.

Her father wasn't finished showing off the countryside. He directed the MMU toward several manufacturing modules where pure crystals of gallium arsenide were made for computer chips and where high-strength metals and temperature-resistant glass were made. "We even have a ball-bearing factory out here," he said. "In zero gravity, we can make perfectly round ball bearings that last almost forever. That was impossible on Earth."

A red-alert light went on in the capsule. "We're at the web. That's about the end of the road," her father said. "All that's out there is the dump—an old asteroid called Phoebe. Not much to see there anyway. And it's not the safest place to be. The Colony is actually surrounded by a kind of electronic grid—like a huge spider web of microwaves—backed up by space-based interceptors. Space debris, asteroids, and other threats are detected and destroyed with lasers before they collide with the Space Colony. It's a little like those bug zappers on Earth. If you need to, you can scan the web for breaks and get through it."

"What sort of other threats are there?" Amelia inquired.

"Space is a big place," her father said. "You never know." Amelia wanted to ask more about this, but her father interrupted her. "How would you like to pilot this? It's really very simple. Basically, the onboard computer will handle it. All you have to do is let the computer know what you want to do. And you can do that through the TAS. It'll probably be easier than maneuvering your wheelchair."

"Can I take us through the web?" Amelia asked. "I'd kind of like to see that asteroid. It sounds mysterious."

"I think we'd better save that for another day," her father said. "It's not really much to see, just a hunk of rock."

Amelia took control of the thrusters and turned the ship around.

The red alert went off as they left the fence or web, or whatever it was, behind. "So take us home," Commander Mann said.

"It feels strange to call that place home," Amelia commented.

"You'll adjust," her father said. "In a way, it's more of a home than Earth. Here, everything was designed with humans in mind. It's actually more centered around our comfort than Earth."

Amelia wasn't so sure. She wondered a little why her father was so anxious to show her everything but was so tight-lipped, almost secretive, about the space dump.

She was, however, getting used to having the TAS thought field humming in her head and was getting better at focusing her own thoughts. But at the same time, she was beginning to sense that her father was shielding his thoughts and feelings about something. Was it just the space dump, or were there other things he was being quiet about?

Back in the Space Station Amelia spoke into her communicator and channeled to Earth, to Gran and Gramps, to the place she really still considered home. She imagined them in their big chairs, bathed in warm, orange light, in front of the flickering wood stove.

"How's our girl?" Gramps asked.

"It's very strange here," Amelia said.

"Goodness, that's to be expected," Gran said. "Living in space would seem a little strange, even to me."

"Actually, it's not so much space," Amelia said thoughtfully. "It's the people. Papa seems secretive, nervous about something. And the kids here are funny. Not funny funny. I mean boring. It's like they all think the same thing. I mean they're all different colors and sizes and everything, but when you hook up to TAS, it's like everybody is the same."

"What's TAS?" Gramps asked, and Amelia explained.

"Interesting," Gran commented.

"I'm trying to fit in," Amelia said. "But it seems kind of boring. They all play the same games—computer simulations of space war."

"The more things change, the more they stay the same," Gramps laughed. "Maybe your being there will make a difference."

Amelia hadn't thought of that. All she really wanted to do was fit in. Well, at least part of her felt that way. "There are like 20,000 Space Cadets," Amelia said. "There's only one of me."

"Sometimes, that's all it takes," Gramps said. "You're special."

"I don't really want to be special," Amelia said. "I would like to be normal."

"You'll grow out of that," Gran joked. "I'm not even sure there is such a thing."

"Besides," Gramps asked, "how could anyone related to Gran be normal?"

"Knock it off, you old codger," Gran said.

Amelia could hear the affection in their teasing. She missed it.

"How's your violin coming?" Gramps asked.

"Still in its case," Amelia said.

"Well, I'd recommend a little Bach or Mozart for soul food," Gran said. "For a contented soul."

"You're really a cabbage butterfly," Gramps said to Amelia. "They never fly straight. 'He lurches here and there by guess, and God, and hope, and hopelessness. Even the aerobatic swift has not his flying-crooked gift.'"

"That's by the poet Robert Graves," Gramps said. "Like the cabbage butterfly, you have a natural talent for flying crooked. And I'm not sure there's that much you can do about it. Or should do about it. People shouldn't deny their gifts."

"Oh, Gramps," Gran said.

"Sorry," Gramps said.

"Amelia will find her own way," Gran said. "That's part of the job of life. But flying crooked gives you more views of the path."

Amelia murmured something vague. She didn't know that soon she would meet someone who was studying insect flight in space, someone about her own age by the name of Thomas Francis. Or that his zigs and zags would make her feel like the proverbial straight arrow.

CHAPTER 5

The Farm Zone, where Commander Stewart lived, became one of Amelia's favorite places. It was a huge tube with a waterfall at one end and fields of potatoes, wheat, corn, and flowers—surrounded by forests of pine, redwood, and oak. It was the part of the Space Station most like Earth and resembled a wide fairy tale valley, except that when you looked up and saw the sky through the sky port, *both* the earth and the moon floated on the horizon.

Amelia had come 240,000 miles to be in a place that resembled pioneer life in the 1800s. Each colonist had about five acres and a small wooden house. The colonists farmed mostly with horses and oxen—using animals made more sense in terms of recycling the precious nutrients, like nitrogen and oxygen, as well as water. The plants, high-tech in their own way, served to filter out carbon dioxide and provide oxygen during the day. For the most part, the Space Cadets avoided this tube. They called it the Salad Machine.

Amelia felt it was more like a time machine, taking the colonists back to a never-never time that was comfortable and familiar. Everything was built to last, or to be re-used, since colonists couldn't just throw things away. There was something very solid and old-fashioned about life in the Farm Zone. It reminded Amelia, pleasantly, of her grandparents.

It was here that Amelia met Thomas Francis.

She was wheeling over a forest path along a creek of clear flowing water, happy that her wheelchair fit so nicely, when she came upon him, kneeling over a trunk of rotting wood.

"Hello," he said, looking up with wide blue eyes. His whole head was wide, and this was accented by his almost white hair and pale eyebrows. There was something moonlike about his face—wide, white, filled with light. He looked about her age.

He held a small plastic collecting bottle. "I'm collecting," he said, holding up his container. "My name is Thomas Francis. Generally, people call me TF."

"I'm Amelia," she said.

"You're new."

"Yes."

"I was born here," TF said.

"Well, nice to meet you," Amelia said. She began maneuvering her wheelchair around him. Something about him made her immediately uncomfortable.

"What happened to your legs?" he asked.

Amelia was startled. Most people wouldn't think of being so direct. TF saw her reaction and said, "Sorry. "

"I was in an accident, two years ago."

TF asked, "What kind of accident?"

"A space-shuttle crash."

"The one in San Francisco in 2058, the collision in which 50 people were killed. I remember."

"So do I. My mother was killed."

"I'm sorry," he said, and Amelia thought she saw him shiver slightly.

"I manage," Amelia said, vaguely irritated.

"Oh, we all manage. These spiders, for example, are remarkably adaptable. I take them back to my lab…."

Amelia interrupted. "You have a lab? You're just a kid."

"I'm just a kid with a lab. It's my father's, actually. I do experiments with the effects of weightlessness on animal behavior mostly. I have studied the behavior of bees and moths in zero gravity. But I do some mechanical tinkering. At the moment, I am studying learning and adaptation in spiders. I am examining how they build webs in zero gravity and how long it takes them to adapt.

"A well-rested spider will learn to spin a web within a day—even though spiders have evolved to depend on gravity and wind to determine web thickness. It's really remarkable. I've also done experiments with bees and cell formation."

"Oh boy," Amelia thought. "This guy is out there. Talk

about a Space Cadet."

"I suppose you've been contacted by the Space Cadets," TF said. Again, he seemed to be following her thoughts. Amelia sensed from his tone of voice that he wasn't overly fond of the cadets.

"Yes, I went through their orientation. I met a couple of them. They didn't like my overalls."

"So you've been brainwashed."

"Please note that I am wearing my overalls today, so I have *not* been brainwashed."

"It's groupthink," TF said. "And they all wander around hooked into that insipid TAS. The Selenians turned it down. They're cranky that way. I want to move there, but, as you said, I'm just a kid."

"Who are the Selenians?" Amelia asked.

"The Lunar Colonists. It goes back to Selene, an old Earth goddess of the moon. My father calls them Lunatics. Did you know Earthers thought the full moon made people crazy? They were right, too. My father, and yours, too, are all anti-moon. My dad works for yours."

Amelia was determined not to ask another question, but wondered why her father hadn't mentioned the Lunar Colonists.

"The Lunar Colonists came first," TF said, "but they were construction workers. They work hard. They provide most of the raw materials for the Space Station and Earth. Their lives are dangerous. Now, they are self-sufficient. They resent sending off their resources but not having a voice in space government."

Amelia was sure her father would not be so unfair.

"Your father has become pompous. He changed when your mother died. My father says he's changed. And now you're here...."

"Stop it," Amelia snapped. Then she softened a little. "I didn't mean to hurt your feelings. I mean by saying you're just a kid."

"No offense taken. I would like you to be my friend."

Amelia was getting used to TF's directness. She answered frankly. "I don't think that is really the kind of thing you decide to do. We just met."

"Let me show you where I live."

Amelia didn't see any harm in that, so TF led her along the forest path toward a clearing where a log cabin stood neatly surrounded by corrals and a rainbow array of flowers.

From a distance, it looked completely normal and Earth-like. But as they approached, Amelia realized that the some of the pastures were miniature versions. The cows and horses were tiny, hardly more than a foot tall.

When she asked TF about this, he asked, "Haven't you wondered how animals were transported here? A cow is a large animal and weighs a lot. They would have been too expensive to bring from Earth. So scientists bred them to be really small, like the ones you see here. Some of them have been bred back to regular size. But some of them are being kept small, maybe for transport to Mars—when the time comes. The trip to Mars is the next big step. And I'm going. I work out every day. Mars has got more gravity than the moon. You have to be in shape."

On one side of the cabin was a garden, and again Amelia was reminded of her grandparents. She recognized green beans, Swiss chard, turnips, broccoli, and herbs like thyme, oregano, and basil.

"It's beautiful," she said.

"There have been studies," TF said. "Psychologists have found that farming makes some people happy. It's good for their souls."

TF was the most peculiar person she had ever met. He was like an old professor in a kid's body. The old man in the moon, she thought.

Inside, the cabin was as rustic and solid as outside. The furniture was rough-hewn from solid wood. She noted, however, that the house was powered by solar cells and that there was a video screen and a computer work station. And for the first time in the Space Station, Amelia saw a collection of books. Just like the ones in her grandparents' home.

"They have their uses" was all Amelia could get TF to say.

The cabin smelled of fresh herbs—rosemary and oregano—hung to dry from the rafters and walls. "I think," TF said, "you and I can be friends."

"We'll see," Amelia said.

Amelia left the cabin and rolled her wheelchair up the

forest path, back to the Whoosh.

"The last thing I need," Amelia thought to herself, "is a weird friend."

6

The message came over Amelia's wrist communicator. From Gran. "We've decided to celebrate our fiftieth on the moon," she said. "Or L5, to be precise."

"What?" Amelia said blankly. She was alone in her room, drifting about, watching an old Western she'd called up from the video library. She was feeling lonely, and it was as if Gran had read her mind. It was perfect timing.

There was a delay of about a second before Gran's voice returned from Earth.

"It was time for a change."

Again, the slight delay. It was a slow-motion dialogue.

"That's wonderful!" Amelia said.

"And we want to do it on L5," Gran added. "So you and Jim can be there. The whole family! What do you think? Honeymoon on the moon. Well, after 50 years, it wouldn't exactly be a honeymoon, but wouldn't it be a hoot?"

"An absolute hoot," Amelia said and laughed. "I never imagined you'd come here, too. I wasn't sure I would see you again."

"Well, Gramps is a strange combination of poet and journalist," Gran said. "Going to the moon again appeals to both parts. I'd like to make the trip at least once. And of course we miss you awfully. I haven't mentioned our plans to Jim yet. I suppose you could tell him. Break it to him gently. He'd probably worry himself to death. What would a couple of nonagenarians do in space?"

"Nonagenarians?" Amelia asked.

"Fancy word for ninety-year-olds," Gran explained. "But tell Jim we're coming. It's difficult to talk to him over the communicator, and he's been a little strange lately. He does seem nervous. Maybe it would be easier for you to talk to him in person."

"I could do that," Amelia said. It was a little strange to hear her father called Jim.

"Well, that's the news from Earth," Gran giggled. "We love you, Amelia."

"I love you too, Grandma," Amelia said. "And Gramps."

"Well, over and out then," Gran said and the communicator clicked off.

Amelia smiled to herself. She couldn't wait to tell her father, to see if the news would erase that hint of sadness that seemed always to play over his features.

She left her cell and took the Whoosh to the hub. Her father had left a message for her that morning that he would be working on Phoebe, the asteroid beyond the web.

"You're Commander Mann's daughter," the port attendant said, checking out a pressure suit for her. P-suits, they called them.

"Yes," Amelia said.

"Well, welcome to L5. Going to do a little exploring?"

"Yes. There's a lot to see."

"Indeed there is. There's a whole universe out there. Of course, I wouldn't recommend you go much beyond the web."

"Maybe just a little," Amelia said. She didn't want to be dishonest. She knew she was going a little beyond where she should. It was like diving alone. You could get away with it if you were careful, but you couldn't do it very often. Besides, ever since that first outing with her father, she had wanted to get a look at the asteroid.

She checked out an MMU and fired up the thrusters, rising from the docking port gently. As her father had said, flying the MMU was almost easier than traveling in her wheelchair. The computer took care of navigating and displayed information on a screen. She could maintain visual control through the viewport, but there was also a scanning screen. You were never very far from news with the onboard video screen. Although the cabin was pressurized, her father had said it was a good idea to wear the pressure suit. "Just in case," he said.

She climbed into the P-suit, including gloves, boots, and helmet. It wasn't that different from scuba gear—basic equipment that kept you alive.

She wanted to surprise her father, so that meant she didn't lock into TAS.

In no time, she passed by the various factory modules and the countless communication satellites, heading in the direction of the moon and of Phoebe. When the alert light went on, she scanned the web, looking for an opening in the microwave pulses. There it was! She zipped through and was now beyond the protective fence.

She felt a moment of fear. She would have to keep sharp watch for asteroids and space debris. Now she was genuinely in the void, and she realized how reassuring TAS could be. She almost put it on but then decided not to. Amelia was not the kind of person to turn back once she had set her mind to something. Now she was on her own. She rather liked the feeling.

She headed toward Phoebe and her father. She had to swerve suddenly to avoid a tiny piece of rock. It showed up on the scanner screen first. An alarm went off, and the scanner screen showed a recommended path for avoiding collision. All Amelia had to do was press the OK button. The computer and the MMU did the rest.

Even a dime-size object could damage the craft if its speed was great enough. What surprised Amelia more was a tiny blue blob, about the size of a quarter, that suddenly glommed onto her viewport. It hadn't even shown up on her scanner. How could that be? Amelia examined it closely. It looked almost exactly like the jellyfish she had seen on her last day on Earth. Surely there weren't any life forms floating out here in space. As she closed in on Phoebe, it vanished, as quickly as it had appeared. She would have to ask her father about it.

There was something sinister about the old asteroid. It was the color of dust, not the bright clean color of the Space Station. She made it to the docking port on Phoebe without further incident and entered the airlock. As she floated out of the MMU, a voice buzzed over her communicator and blue alarm lights flashed around her. "Please identify yourself and purpose of visit."

"I'm here to see my father, Commander Mann."

"Log shows no authorization," the voice buzzed with static. At the same time, the voice was warm, motherly, and stern. Amelia realized she was talking to a computer.

"It's a surprise visit," Amelia said. "It's very important."

There was a pause in the communicator's transmission.

Then a familiar voice came over the communicator. "Amelia, what on Earth are you doing here?"

"Papa! I have news I have to tell you. Where are you?"

"Stay where you are. I'll be right there."

The alarms stopped flashing, but Amelia felt distinctly unwelcome. Minutes later, her father's stern look did little to lift the feeling.

"Amelia, Phoebe is strictly off-limits. You had to pass through the web. This place is extremely dangerous. Only authorized personnel are allowed here—you know that."

"I'm sorry, Papa. I had to see you."

"What could be so important that you risked your life? That you violated Space Station security? Amelia! "

"Papa, Gran and Gramps are coming!"

Her father's expression softened only slightly. "Amelia, you could have used your communicator."

"I was too happy. I wanted to see your face. I thought you would be happy. Our whole family will be together for their fiftieth anniversary."

"I *am* happy. But that's not the point. You might have been killed."

"But I wasn't. Like you said, flying the MMU is easy. "

"Again, that's not the point. This visit was extremely foolish. I will have to take you back. Immediately."

Without pausing or offering to show Amelia anything beyond the docking port, Commander Mann hooked the two MMUs together and had Amelia join him in his. They sat in uncomfortable silence for most of the trip back to the Space Station. Even locked into TAS, almost no thoughts passed between them. Amelia wanted to ask him about the little space jellyfish she had seen but didn't. She thought that the less said about her trip, the better things would be.

"Amelia, I'm sorry to be so harsh," her father said finally taking off the TAS phones. "But you're the only thing I have left since your mother died. You are so precious to me. I don't know what I would do if I lost you. I don't mean to be cruel. I'm not angry. I suppose I am frightened—frightened that you might have been hurt or worse. We live in an unforgiving environment. We have to be very careful. Do you understand what I am saying?"

"Yes, Papa. I'm sorry. I guess I feel the same way. I was so happy. But I was also suddenly very lonely."

Commander Mann looked at his daughter. The sadness was still there in his face. "We will have to have a long talk soon," he said. "We have been apart so long, and so much has changed. I need to sort out a few things first." He reached across the cockpit and gently laid his hand on Amelia's long red hair.

The next morning, TF called her early over her communicator, but Amelia didn't answer. The communicator also recorded messages. Today she planned to take an MMU and explore by herself. This time, she wouldn't go near the web, but she was curious about those "jellyfish."

Once out of the docking port, Amelia put the MMU through its paces. It was rather like a souped-up wheelchair, and she zipped through space, doing somersaults. She didn't imagine her father would approve. Amelia again left off the TAS earphones, since she was going to be good, sort of. Then she settled down and cruised past the factory modules, all abuzz with MMU traffic, to the communication satellites and the solar power station.

It was at one of the communication satellites that the jellyfish appeared again, except this time, there wasn't just one strange creature. There was a school of the delicate beings floating along. As they attached themselves to her viewport, Amelia had a chance to really examine them. They were very much like the jellyfish she had known on Earth—light blue, transparent, and equipped with a fin and tentacles. But what good would a fin do in this windless environment? And what would the tentacles catch? There was also a little solid rectangle embedded in the blue plasticlike substance. These were very mysterious creatures indeed. Since they didn't seem particularly threatening. Amelia decided to try to capture one for study.

Using the MMU's mechanical arm, she managed to clamp one of the jellyfish and transfer it to the intake port. It took several tries with the metal fingers of the arm.

Now what? She could see the jellyfish floating in the chamber. Should she return to the Space Station and study it there? Or why not look at it right now? Amelia decided to open the airlock and bring the jellyfish in.

But when Amelia opened the clamped door on the pressure chamber, the jellyfish moved with surprising speed, like a lizard. It headed straight to the onboard computer and attached itself.

Within seconds, the MMU altered course and headed toward the web. Amelia tried to pry the thing off her dashboard, but it wouldn't budge. It pulsed with energy, and Amelia saw her screen doing strange things. Whole programs flashed there and disappeared. A jagged line of green light crossed the screen like lightning.

Amelia tugged at the creature again, and this time it popped free and turned on her. Even through her glove she felt sharp pain shooting up her arm. In a panic, she shook it free. The force of her own motion sent her tumbling around the cabin. She smacked sharply into a bank of equipment. Red and blue alert lights flashed all around the cabin.

Amelia gasped from fear and pain.

Meanwhile the jellyfish immediately attached itself to the computer. And again the ship took off toward the web, accelerating.

The red alert-light went on as the ship hurtled into the web, not bothering to scan for an opening. Laser beams flashed from the interceptors, and Amelia felt the jolt of energy hit her MMU. But it continued on toward Phoebe. Amelia had to do something! She searched the cabin for some kind of tool, some kind of weapon. There it was!

She reached for the onboard laser gun that was clamped to the capsule's wall. She pulled it free and aimed with both hands at the creature who had taken over her computer. She had never even held such a gun. She squinted. She fired.

And missed. Which was no wonder. Her hands were shaking from fear and the pain of the sting. She had left a jagged hole of smoking metal in the instrument panel.

She aimed again, a little to the left.

And missed again. Too far to the left. Out of the corner of her eye she saw an interceptor from out the viewport. Would the ship be destroyed before she could get control?

She moved closer. She concentrated and steadied herself against the top of the cabin. She took a deep breath and pulled the trigger again.

A thin line of ruby-red light turned the jellyfish into a smudge of ash. The ship slowed and Amelia took another deep breath. At the same time, the interceptor veered away. Maybe they didn't chase things too far outside the web. But what exactly had happened? Had she damaged the computer? Would she be able to navigate back through the web?

Maybe now it was time for TAS. She put on the earphones, but the system was dead. So was the navigation screen. She tried the hydrogen thrusters but they didn't respond. She was drifting in space, beyond the web. A thought came to her: She was as good as dead.

Suddenly a voice came over her communicator. "Amelia! Amelia?" It was TF. "Are we having fun yet?" he asked.

"Oh, TF!" Amelia almost screamed. "Everything's gone. Power. Computer. Everything."

"Not to worry," TF said. "If you look out your viewport, I'm right above you. I saw you take in the jellyfish. Not smart, that. Those guys will eat up your communications."

"What do I do now?" Amelia said.

"No problem, really," TF said. "We'll dock. And I'll tow

you back through the web and so on. We don't have much time to waste."

Seconds later, Amelia felt TF's MMU lock onto hers with a clunk. Over the communicator, he told her to join him in his capsule. "I don't know how long your cabin pressure will last. Or anything else."

The pressure port hissed open, and Amelia floated out of her capsule, closing it behind her. Then she opened the other door and drifted up into TF's capsule.

She took another deep breath, realizing that she had hardly been breathing except for occasional gasps. She was safe. Through his helmet visor, Amelia saw a smile spread across his moonlike face. "I still think we can be friends," he said.

"You saved my life" was all Amelia could think to say.

"You probably could have used your communicator," TF said.

"Yes, but it would have been too late."

"Then you don't mind that I followed you?"

Amelia hadn't even considered that until now. "How'd you know where I was?"

"I just had a feeling," TF said. "Just an idea."

TF maneuvered the ships around and headed back toward the web. "Let's get out of here," he said. "There's something alive in this darkness. Besides the blue meanies."

They made it back through the web and to the hub of the

Space Colony without incident. TF examined the cabin of Amelia's MMU. He played with the computer console a moment. "We'll probably have to file a report, although we might be able to get around it if I can repair the damage," TF said. "Maybe I could transfer the program from my MMU. I don't think the jellyfish actually hurt the hardware. This shouldn't take too long."

"What are they?" Amelia asked. "Are those things alive?"

"They're not alive. They're small, clever robots. They're kind of hard to capture. They glom onto computers. My father—and yours—think they were created by the Moon Folk to attack communication satellites.

"Fiddlesticks!" Amelia burst out with a favorite Grampsism. "That doesn't make sense at all."

"Yeah. They clearly have a computer chip inside. Maybe they're made of old rocket fuel and plasma. So the questions are *who, what, why,* and *where*? And the answer to the *where* is Phoebe. That's where all that stuff is stored. As to the rest, I'm working on it. Care to join me in the lab? I have a theory."

"Which is?" Amelia asked.

"Mother hen. Her little chicks," TF intoned.

"Let's see if I can translate," Amelia said briskly. "There's a big momma out there, sending her little babies out into danger. That's wrong. Mothers don't do that."

TF stared at her, and then somehow made a sweeping old-fashioned bow, without tumbling all over the place.

"You are so right. Wrong metaphor, wrong thought.

More like a queen bee, making specialized creatures—drones, soldiers—as the need arises. The first need is…?"

"Food. Always." As the daughter of a biologist, Amelia had no doubt about that.

"Aha!" cried TF. Then, earnestly, almost begging, he said, "You must come to the lab with me."

"We also need to take another look at these jellyfish," Amelia said.

"Yes," TF said. "Or we could let the adults handle it. I know they have their own theories and their own solutions."

"Like what?" Amelia asked.

"War."

"Pish and tosh!" Amelia found herself falling back on another Grampsism.

"Question," barked TF. "The war games the Space Cadets play. Why do they play them?"

"I see what you're saying," Amelia answered, shocked to her core. "Those clones wouldn't do something that wasn't approved. Like puppies playing, to learn everything they need to know as grown-up dogs."

"My father thinks the Lunars want to get at the Space Colony's communications system. Ask your father."

"I'm not sure he'd tell me anything," Amelia said.

"Having some danger out there makes for a nice team spirit, competition, bonding. It sort of happened to us, sort of."

"Thomas Francis, you're weird," Amelia pronounced

with all the certainty she could muster. "But the Cadets are weirder, so we'd better check out your lab," she finished a bit lamely.

"Thank you," TF said. It seemed to come from somewhere deep inside. Then he squinted at her and said in a lighter tone, "Hey, good shot in there. Play any war games lately?"

Amelia took a quick, sharp swipe at him, and TF ducked with genuine alarm. When you don't weigh anything at all, violent movements send you flopping around like balloons. And as Amelia and TF tumbled in opposite directions, they both giggled and then screamed with a laughter that flowed like tears.

That evening, after tea with TF, Amelia found a note on her screen. It said "I need to talk with you about a disturbing report from the Space Cadets. Dad."

Amelia realized that the Space Cadets had somehow found out about her narrow escape. More and more, she was beginning to agree with TF about that group.

She entered through the door that connected their two cells and heard him talking. She called out "Papa," but he didn't hear her. It sounded like a serious conversation.

"They've got the fusion reactors and the mass drivers," Commander Mann was saying. "They're definitely a threat. Plus they control our supplies of oxygen, helium 3, and water. Now they're taunting us with those jellyfish. My people have found them on the solar collector and clogging the communication satellites. We haven't been able to capture one. They are incredibly elusive. But there are thousands of them. In essence, we've been attacked. Liz, we have to consider our options. I wouldn't rule out a first strike."

Amelia heard Elizabeth Stewart's calm voice respond. "Jim, talk about first strikes is premature. We have to talk to Thor. I can't believe he'd do anything hostile without talking to us first. We depend on him and the colonists, but they also depend on us. Where would they be without the lunar transports? They couldn't survive without those supplies."

Jim responded: "Thor is a troublemaker, and you know it. He's got the colonists all worked up. They're talking independence. They want more power. Maybe they've developed another supply route. I'm beginning to feel like King George the Third."

Commander Stewart laughed. "Well, he was mad," she said. "You're not mad. Right, Jim?"

"Recently, I'm not so sure. But, no, I'm not. But I'm not sure you're taking this threat seriously."

"I'm taking it very seriously, Jim," Elizabeth said. And Amelia thought that she sounded very serious. "Threatening force is not my way of taking things seriously, as you well know. That's a last resort and could destroy everything we've built. We depend on them. They depend on us. We will have to talk."

"Those jellyfish are more than talk."

"We need more information, less guesswork. And less war paint," Elizabeth snapped. "We're not sure where they come from, are we?"

"It's a reasonable guess," Jim said. "They're definitely designed. Designed for destruction. Who else has a motive?"

"You tell me, Commander. You're supposed to be my systems guru."

Commander Mann turned and saw Amelia. "Elizabeth, may we talk later," he said. "My daughter is here."

"Give her my love," Elizabeth said. "In the meantime, I will arrange for a meeting with Thor."

Commander Mann clicked off his communicator and turned to his daughter.

Amelia shrugged her shoulders, embarrassed to be caught eavesdropping but fascinated by what she had just heard. TF was right. They were talking war.

She was floating in the middle of her father's living room. There was nothing soft about it, nothing comfortable. There was a map of the moon and a map of Phoebe on the walls.

"Amelia!" her father said. "How's my girl? I just got the safety report from the hub. But other than that, how are you?"

"I'm getting used to it. And I have met a friend, Thomas Francis."

Amelia thought her father would be sterner. The note he'd left sounded stern.

"I know TF and his parents," Jim said. "His father, Cap, and I work together. I understand that you and TF ran into a little trouble today. And I needed to talk to you. The Space Cadets notified me that you took an MMU beyond the web.

They said you weren't locked into TAS and that there was damage to the ship. They monitor activity that isn't TAS locked. They want people hooked up to TAS. It's for your own safety. "

"Those little beasts!" Amelia cried and added, "It wasn't my fault. I didn't have any choice. One of those jellyfish— or whatever they are—took over the ship. It took me through the web. It was out of control. I had to shoot it. It was scary."

"Once again," her father said, "you could have been killed. Amelia, you're going to give me a nervous breakdown! Couldn't you stay in the Space Colony and practice violin? Or start a garden? Something a little safer?"

"I suppose," Amelia said. She thought but didn't say that she would do anything to make him happier. She wasn't sure what the problem was.

"Are you really upset?" she asked, knowing that her father seemed more depressed than angry.

Her dad shook his head. "I have explained to you how precious you are to me. That's part of the reason I was so harsh. But there's more.

"I was very much in love with your mother," her dad continued. "She was beautiful and brave and very bright. It startles me how much you have come to look like her. I see her reflected in your eyes, in your hair. I can't help but think of her when I look at you."

Amelia's father was not speaking with his usual certainty. He did not sound like the same commander who had just suggested some sort of strike against the Lunar Colonists.

He wasn't sure how much of this Amelia would understand. Growing up, he thought Gramps and Gran were scatterbrained hippies. He wanted to do hard science and be focused. And he became a man who was too focused sometimes. Margaret could always nudge him onto other tracks, make him think about the longer, slower, deeper wavelengths. When she died, he should have come home to stay. He was not one of those men who could solve grief by working, by staying on the job. But then those jellyfish appeared. He was missing something. Not only about the jellyfish and the job. He was missing something he needed to be whole.

He dragged his fingers through his hair and spoke slowly and softly. "I still miss Margaret. I tried to just forget that whole part of my life. I thought I had. I thought I could start over, but I can't. I think facing up to the sadness is really the only way to get over it. Sometimes I'm not sure I'm thinking entirely straight. Even about things that aren't related to your mother."

"That's all right, Papa," Amelia said. "I miss Gramps and Gran, too. But not like Mom."

"No, not like Mom." He corrected himself. "Not like Margaret."

Amelia was surprised to see her father's icy blue eyes water with tears. Then she remembered, you couldn't control tears. Not even her father, a space commander, could. It shocked her that her father needed someone to take care of him. Or that he sensed he was failing to do his job properly.

Amelia said, "Oh, Papa," and began to cry also.

They floated, tears streaming down their cheeks.

Except that, of course, the tears didn't exactly stream. In zero gravity, they formed into little balls and floated like tiny salt-water bubbles. Soon they were getting into both Amelia's and her father's ears, which tickled. The next thing they knew, they were giggling. Then they went silent again for a few moments.

"Well," he said finally. "That wasn't really fair. You have enough on your plate."

"After all," Amelia said. "I'm just a kid."

"Perhaps," Jim said, "after your wicked adventure, you'd like to join me for a little real food at Elizabeth's. We're invited."

That, to Amelia, seemed like a marvelous idea.

"I have taken the liberty of inviting TF and his family," Jim said. "Maybe you would like to bring your violin."

There were only the six of them. The mood was not as grand as Amelia's first dinner at Elizabeth's, but it was just as good. Again, all the fruits and vegetables—quash, corn, oranges, and even a watermelon—were fresh. Purple, blue, and yellow flowers were arranged in the middle of the table. Dessert was apples, oranges, and melons, all carefully sliced in crescents, like quarter moons. There was more tea— a buttery brew that TF's mother, Lillian, had brought. "It's chamomile, with a secret ingredient" she explained with a wink.

Both TF's father and mother had blond hair and pale skin, though darker than TF's. His father said very little but looked strong and practical. He worked with her dad in environmental management. TF's mother was a botanist and a midwife. She had delivered many of the babies born in the Space Station. She had written papers on the medicinal uses of herbs and roots.

"It's good for lowering blood pressure," TF said of the tea. "Mother thought…."

"Which, thanks to you two," her dad interrupted, "I am about to develop. My only daughter has been in space three days, and she's already laser blasting. That's something, by the way, I have yet to do as a Space Commander. Except, of course, on the practice range."

Amelia's father paused and cleared his throat. He continued: "I know the Space Cadets can be a little overly zealous, but they have raised some interesting points. Why weren't you hooked into TAS, especially beyond the web? What on earth were you doing out there laser blasting your MMUs? The Space Cadets have actually suggested reprimands and restrictions. Exactly what happened?"

TF and Amelia looked at each other. For a moment, they exchanged thoughts. Or at least Amelia felt that they had. She felt that TF wanted her to explain.

"We didn't mean to go beyond the web," Amelia

explained again. "I saw these weird jellyfishlike things. And I've seen them once before. They reminded me of the jellyfish I'd seen on Earth. So I decided to study one—as my mother used to do. When I captured one, it took over the ship. It just stuck right onto the computer controls and wouldn't let go. It stung me. And it took the ship right through the web. What are they?"

"We're not entirely sure," Commander Mann said—rather stiffly, Amelia thought. His mood had changed since just a few minutes ago in his cabin.

"What we do know at this point is highly confidential," he said. "And it feels rather strange to be discussing top-secret material with two kids. That, too, could contribute to high blood pressure."

Around Elizabeth, Amelia thought her father seemed to relax a little. He issued statements like a commander but then tried to be a little bit funny. Amelia liked the effect Elizabeth had on her father.

It was Elizabeth who said, "They appear to be manufactured rather than actual life forms. And it is peculiar that you managed to capture one. Our scientists have been unsuccessful. Isn't that right, Jim?"

Commander Mann cleared his throat again. "That is why I think it might be worthwhile to discuss these jellyfish with you two. You seem to have an in with these creatures. Why have our crews been unable to capture one of these strange creatures?"

"TAS has something to do with it," Amelia said. "I wasn't hooked up to TAS. I wanted to feel what it was like without a thousand other voices in my head."

"Well, obviously, Space Colony security isn't much of a concern to you," Commander Mann said. "But I wouldn't mind feeling just a bit secure from time to time. I wouldn't mind my own daughter accommodating this need just a bit," he said softly as the adults chuckled.

"But maybe the jellyfish avoid TAS," Amelia said. "It has a pretty complicated security system, doesn't it? Maybe the jellyfish can't deal with that."

"More tea?" TF's mother asked.

The conversation veered away from jellyfish. Amelia was disappointed. It seemed that she and TF actually knew more about the jellyfish than the Space Colony's leaders.

After dinner, Amelia wheeled away from the table and pulled her violin from its case. The strings had all gone loose so she needed to tune the violin. She rosined her bow.

Slowly, she began a Bach sonata from memory. The rich chords floated in the hall like huge beams, creating a structure of sound. She floated there. Everything was connected and flowing.

Playing the violin was what she had been doing for the last two years on Earth, how she had been using the long afternoons alone since her accident. Practicing scales and exercises had taken her mind off the accident and the pain. Gradually, she had started playing real music—Bach and Mozart and Beethoven.

Violin had given her something to do when she was recovering. She practiced three to five hours a day. Taking lessons once a week, she had gotten quite good. To most of the kids in her school, playing violin was a little bit strange—it was old-fashioned.

Now, she could see her grandparents' tiny living room again. She imagined Gramps with his flowing gray hair and bushy beard. He used to kind of hum along with the Bach, in a gruff way. She could see Gran's eyes sparkling like jewels in the firelight.

Memory could come up with all sorts of things—from Bach to Gramps.

"I'm getting pretty sappy here," she said to herself and launched into a fast, crisp second movement, each note like cut glass.

The applause brought Amelia out of her reverie.

"That was marvelous," Elizabeth said. Jim still sat with his eyes closed and a smile on his lips. Cap, TF's father, was staring upwards. TF's mother sat leaning forward with bright, wide eyes. Music affected people in different ways.

"Bach to Bach," TF quipped and sat down next to Amelia with a cello, much to her surprise. He played an unaccompanied cello sonata, also from memory. Amelia was astonished. He dipped down into the rich, dark tones the violin never ventured into. He soared on the high notes. All the time she had been practicing on Earth, he had been up here working, too. They had been companions before she even knew he existed. She wondered what memories the music brought back for him. She remembered a nursery rhyme from her early childhood: "I see the moon, the moon sees me. The moon sees somebody I want to see."

This time, Amelia led the applause, in a bit of a daze.

"That music will never, ever lose its power," Lillian said. "Even if we get to Mars, there will be room for Bach and Mozart!"

"*When* we get to Mars," TF chirped, looking a bit miffed.

The grownups then talked about the space exploration budget cuts, how unlikely it was that the next step—the settlement on Mars—would ever really be achieved.

"I would love to go to Mars. It would be strangely familiar," Commander Stewart said. "The day is only 40 minutes longer than Earth's. And there is some atmosphere, even if the skies are pink instead of blue. Even if its gravity is only a third of Earth's.

"Imagine a mountain over fifteen miles high or a canyon five miles deep!" TF exclaimed. "They make Mount Everest and the Grand Canyon look puny."

"Plenty to do right here," murmured TF's father. "Keeping a whole artificial world running."

Amelia learned the long-range plan was to build enclosed colonies much like those on the moon. They would be constructed from brick, mortar, and plastic made from

Martian soil. Scientists had hoped to have a colony of 150 people on Mars by the year 2065. That was only five years away.

In the really long term, scientists hoped to gradually change Mars into a more Earth-like environment—making it warmer and wetter and safer. This would involve pumping the atmosphere full of gases to raise the temperature. Then Mars's ice would melt. TF's father thought that the planet could support insects, plants, and perhaps humans in just a few decades. Of course, all that would take huge amounts of money.

"Well, at the very least," Jim said, "we ought to have robots out there collecting samples so that we know what we're dealing with. Right now, there's not even money in the budget for that. We're losing the last frontier."

Commander Stewart beamed at him. "Find us a way," she said. "I know you can."

Then, switching gears, she announced, "I have made arrangements with Thor. We will travel to the moon to talk with him."

Commander Mann nodded. "Most likely, we will wind up listening to him," he said.

"He has some valid complaints," Elizabeth commented.

As though thinking out loud, TF's father said, "Maybe we should give him something to really complain about."

CHAPTER

8

TF's voice chimed bright and sunny over the communicator and woke Amelia in her cell. Many mornings, Amelia thought, began with a call from TF!

"I think we may get a chance to go to the moon," he said without saying hello. "When the bigwigs go to talk with Thor, they don't want to look hostile. My father said they're considering taking some kids along. Like a big family outing. Have you heard anything?"

"No," Amelia said, still a little groggy with sleep. "Papa hasn't mentioned it."

"But you'd want to go?"

"I suppose," Amelia said. "It feels like I just got here. I might not want to go."

"Why not?" TF asked.

"A couple more ten-hour trips?" Amelia asked, feeling

rather ornery.

"Yeah, yeah. We'd probably take the OTV."

"English, please!"

"The Orbital Transfer Vehicle. We could see the moon observatory and the oxygen mines. And the fusion reactor. We'd be on the frontier, Amelia! In scientific thought and actual space."

"I thought I was there already," Amelia said.

"No, it's different on the moon," TF insisted. "The spirit's different. For one thing, there's no TAS. The Lunies actually voted against it."

Amelia liked that. She said she would ask her father about the trip.

"You might have to do more than ask," TF said. "I don't think our parents really want us to go. That was Commander Stewart's idea. You might have to persuade your father a little."

"I'll try," Amelia said. "I'll talk to him during the exercise cycle."

For people who lived in the zero or partial-gravity zones, an hour a day of exercise on a treadmill and an exercise bicycle was required by Space Station rules. Otherwise, work in the outer zones could cause muscle cramps or worse. Amelia was used to exercising every day. It had been part of her recovery. "You have to keep these up," her doctor had told her. "The blood must flow, not sit there."

Amelia got to the gym early, strapped her feet into the

pedals, and clicked the bicycle on. The cycle actually moved her muscles for her while she worked her arms and back muscles on the oarlike handlebars. This was necessary to maintain circulation and keep all sorts of dreadful things from happening, including gangrene.

The screen provided a variety of virtual reality tapes to exercise with. You basically entered the consciousness of an animal. You could be a cheetah stalking its prey or wild horses running on the prairie. Amelia chose a tape of a shark, always swimming, its streamlined form slicing through turquoise water. She liked the combination of energy and coolness.

Her father appeared shortly after Amelia had begun exercising.

"Hello," he said simply.

Dressed in baggy sweat clothes, her father sat down next to Amelia on an exercise bicycle. He began pedaling at a furious pace.

He didn't watch films as he exercised. He moved from the bicycle to the bench press and then the leg lifts. He worked quickly at each station, allowing only 15 seconds between sets.

"I'm afraid I lost it a little yesterday afternoon," he said. "I didn't mean to unload on you. Children should be free of adult concerns. Children should be allowed to be children. But you do bring back memories of Margaret and of our life together. The past confuses the present.

"Elizabeth says I need a vacation, and I agree, actually.

But right now, there just isn't time. We've got those jellyfish to deal with. And there's the Mars mission that demands attention, just to get funding. Meanwhile, I'm thinking of Margaret, something I thought I had put behind me. Honestly, sometimes I just feel confused."

"I liked it that tears floated like raindrops," Amelia said, "And tickled.

"Are we going to the moon?" she blurted out. It wasn't exactly the subtle approach she had planned.

"Well, doesn't news travel fast?" her dad said. Amelia could tell he wasn't pleased by the question. "Commander Stewart has asked that you accompany us in a mission. I don't think it's a particularly good idea. But we're going to talk to Thor, and Elizabeth wanted you to come. You and TF. You don't mind being used as pawns?"

"Pawns?"

"I can't tell you all that's going on. That would be inappropriate. There are security matters involved. But Liz feels that children would soften our message to Thor and the Lunar Colonists. I don't think our message should be softened. But she's the boss. She may be right. You and TF are the only ones who've seen the jellyfish up close. And those little robots are at the center of our problems with the Lunar Colonists."

"I'd like to go," Amelia pronounced, as though she was not going to take no for an answer.

"I am surrounded by strong women," Jim said, and actually laughed.

"I guess the problems with the Lunar Colonists are pretty serious," Amelia added.

"We wouldn't be going to the moon if they weren't," Jim said. "But I think we can work things out. In any case, it should be interesting for you. They're a different breed."

The journey from the Space Colony to the moon was quite different from Amelia's journey from Earth to the Space Colony—although it was about the same number of miles. For one thing, TF sat next to her. They played chess on a small magnetic board. It occurred to Amelia that chess was a war game. Knights and castles and pawns all were involved in getting at the king and queen.

"Do you think we're pawns?" Amelia asked. "I mean, in this Lunar Colony thing. What are we supposed to do?"

"Kids have their uses," TF said. "But I don't think we're being used. Commander Stewart wouldn't do that. We do have a role, however. Don't forget, we're the only ones who have been able to examine a jellyfish. Maybe we'll get to talk about them. And maybe somebody will listen."

Amelia found that in chess, which she had learned from Gramps, TF was just about unbeatable. During one game, TF said, "I think your father is a little jealous of Thor."

"What?" Amelia asked. "Why?" This idea floored her. Once again, she had trouble ignoring TF's moon face and separating what he was saying from his chirpy voice.

"Thor and Commander Stewart were both Lunar Colonists. They go way back. Your father is in love with Commander Stewart. How would you like Thor as a rival?"

"This is very complicated," Amelia said, overwhelmed. She had seen the same thing, but she hadn't really put the pieces together. In the clear, cold part of her mind, it clicked. "I'm just a kid," she teased. She knew TF was right, as usual. But it seemed like too much to consider.

"Do you think they will get married?" Amelia asked.

"I wouldn't be surprised," TF said.

"This is serious," Amelia said."It would be nice— strange, but nice."

"I think so too," TF said. "You should develop your knights and bishops earlier. You hang back in mid-game."

TF moved his bishop, protected by two knights, into a space threatening Amelia's queen and king. Checkmate was only a move away. TF won again.

"See what I mean?" he asked. "You have to take control of the board." Playing against TF was a little like playing against a computer. She'd done that before, with the same dismal results.

From space, the moon looked gray, the color of oil-stained concrete. The OTV landed in the center of a large crater and taxied into a huge hangar. The inhabitants of the Lunar Colonies lived in large bubbles—transparent enclosures miles long and 1,600 feet high. The largest part of the bubbles were buried deep into the rock of the moon. Mirrors and filters bent light to make the insides of these enclosures Earth-like. The atmosphere inside was completely artificial—a delicate balance of oxygen, carbon dioxide, and nitrogen. These gases were mined from moon rock and pumped into the life-supporting spaces.

The Lunar Colony was like skyscrapers sunk down into levels packed with entire families and contained schools, stores, businesses and government offices. But it struck Amelia as all rather stark and gray and dusty, with no frills.

What really startled Amelia, however, was how tall everyone was. TF explained that the moon's gravity was about a sixth of the Earth's. People grew taller here. Even people just visiting for a week could gain an inch or two in height. "People who grew up here can easily get to be seven or eight feet tall," TF said. "With so little gravity, their spines relax. They're big, but they're weaker than Earth people. Most of these people couldn't go back to Earth. They'd be crushed by one G. They're moon people. Not one of them wants to go back."

TF explained that, seven years ago, the Lunies voted to give up Earth time. "They were creating artificial 24-hour, day-and-night cycles. Now they're on the moon's natural cycle. A moon day lasts two Earth weeks. And then come two weeks of night. The real radicals try to stay up the whole two weeks. They tend to get a little grumpy."

The moon was utterly dead. It had no air or water, no wind or rain or snow. It was as still and dusty as a billion-year-old tomb. There was no sound. Everything was either very hot or very cold. TF said that temperatures ranged from 265 degrees Fahrenheit during the long days to −310 degrees Fahrenheit during the night—both lethal to human, animal, or plant life.

But for Amelia, there was something oddly comforting about the moon. Nothing changed. Craters and rocks she saw now had sat there for millions, maybe billions, of years. Just about everything was covered with a layer of moon dust. It was like snow piled up over millions of years. In some places, TF told her, the dust was 60 feet thick.

Over objections from both Jim and TF's father, Elizabeth invited Amelia and TF to the meeting scheduled with Thor and the community of Lunar Colonists. "I think having young people there will help civilize the goings-on," she said. "Besides, it's the children's future we're talking about. If these talks fall through, who will be affected more than the young people on the moon and in the Space Station?"

Jim clenched his jaw but did not argue.

The meeting was to be held in the Sea of Tranquillity. This was not a sea at all, but a huge crater created about 3 billion years ago and flooded with lava, now hardened and glassy. Early astronomers like Galileo mistakenly thought that the flat spaces on the moon were seas and named them the Sea of Showers and the Sea of Serenity. Inside the large craters were many smaller craters, formed when meteorites hit the moon's surface. There was no atmosphere to burn up the meteorites as on Earth. Yes, Amelia thought, the moon was an unprotected place. It seemed dangerous. Even the Sea of Tranquillity.

The Lunar Colonists had built one of their largest complexes in the Sea of Tranquillity. Most of the government and business of the moon took place here. There were also research centers—among the first built on the moon.

Commander Stewart and her companions were escorted to a large dome made of cement blocks and diamond-hard glass. To Amelia, it looked something like a giant igloo with skylights.

"Lizzie, over here!" a huge voice bellowed out as they entered the hall. "Howdy Do!"

The voice belonged to the largest man Amelia had ever seen. He was literally a giant. He was at least eight feet tall, and he wasn't thin like most of the Lunar Colonists. He enveloped Elizabeth in his huge arms, making her look like a child. Then he grasped Jim's hand in both of his, like a small boy's. When introduced to Amelia, he simply lifted her to where he could see her face and gave her big kisses on both cheeks, tickling her with his beard. He lowered her gently back into her wheelchair. Despite what TF had said about the Lunies being weaker than Earthlings, Amelia knew that this man was like a forklift.

Thor lived up to the name of the old Norse god of thunder. This is what gods looked like. He had a great red beard and a long braid that nearly reached his waist.

He moved like a tiger. The rest of them, except for Elizabeth, walked a little awkwardly, occasionally bouncing several feet off the ground. Amelia stayed in her wheelchair but sensed that traction was not too good.

"It is good to see our neighbors!" he said. "And Lizzie, my love! How long has it been? A year or two at least?"

He hugged Commander Stewart again and swung her in a wide circle. "We grew up together," he explained to Amelia and TF, who both looked a little startled."We went to the Lunar Academy together. In fact, our families go back two generations on the moon."

Commander Mann looked grim.

Commander Stewart smiled. "You stay the same."

"Like moon dust!" Thor said. "The winds of change hardly blow on the moon, eh Commander Jim?"

"That's a matter of some debate," Jim said.

"Yes, indeed," Thor said. "But the debate can wait. First, I have to show you my newest pride and joy. You will appreciate this, Amelia. Your dear ma, Maggie May, was very much a part of its beginnings."

"You mean Margaret," Jim said.

"Right, what a horrible loss that was. Dear, dear Maggie. An incredible biologist."

Thor turned on his heels and bounded into a large hallway. The group followed, some of them—Jim and TF's father Cap—rather reluctantly. They weren't used to being herded around or following anyone else. Commander Stewart, however, didn't seem to mind.

"Still the showman," Jim said under his breath. The hallway led to a huge room bathed in pale blue-green light. The walls were lined with gigantic gurgling tanks. To Amelia, it looked very much like the labs where her mother had worked in Pacific Grove, only it was very much bigger.

"These started out as plankton tanks," Thor boomed. "With the help of your ma and other biologists, we were looking into raising plankton as food. I remember we joked that we were dealing with broccoli doing the breast stroke, but your mother took it seriously. These were the prototype plankton ponds, where we raised the first batches. It worked so well, we had to expand to larger ponds. It's amazing what a creative chef can do with a bunch of slime. Very high protein. But aren't these grand?"

Thor clapped his huge hands, and it was impossible not to share his enthusiasm. Giant anemones and seaweed swayed in some of the tanks, which stretched several stories. Other tanks held schools of tiny silver and blue fish—anchovies, Amelia guessed. Sharks floated lazily in another large tank.

"This is just like home!" Amelia cried.

Thor thundered with warm laughter. "Exactly, my child. Just like home. My scientists have created a habitat very much like Earth's. I have specimens from just about every marine environment on Earth. There are fish here from freshwater lakes and rivers in Africa and South America. The reduced gravity hasn't actually proved a problem for my pets. They adjust, if you give them time—just like all of us living creatures."

"Where on earth did all this come from?" Jim asked. "I don't recall seeing the paperwork at the Space Colony. Where are the receipts and orders?"

Thor cleared his throat. "Well, yes. After the plankton ponds, this became more of a moon-based project. I didn't burden the Space Colony with a lot of paperwork. Some of what you see was transported more as special presents. Special requests. My visitors know what makes me happy. A shark egg case, a sea urchin, a strand of kelp. It has taken some time and much generosity."

"Quite a bit of generosity, I'd say," Jim said.

"Do you have something against the kindness of friends? Or even strangers, Commander Mann?" Thor mumbled, seeming to wait for a reply. When none came, he cheered and continued. "Of course, we have done some very valuable research in the meantime. And we continue to harvest plankton as well as fish. Commander, you should see the abalone we grow here! Delicious. They grow wonderfully in reduced gravity, and you don't have to pound them so much!"

"I'd like to see the balance sheet," Jim said. "I suspect that a profit-and-loss statement would be educational."

"Commander, life can't be lived around decimal points," Thor pronounced. "Cynics see the cost of everything, the value of nothing! The frontier is hardly the place for cynicism. Cynicism is a luxury we can't afford."

Stretching his arms wide, Thor herded them to another

small tank, where a chambered nautilus floated. Its huge unblinking eye seemed to watch them. "Slowly, this beautiful animal has filled its chambers with gas as it has grown," Thor said. "So now it floats in a lunar sea, perfectly balanced, responding not to Earth's gravity but to the moon's. I could watch it for hours! After hours working in the mines, our workers come here just to unwind and to wonder. Isn't there wonder here, Commander Mann?"

"And do you raise jellyfish as well?" Jim asked.

Thor looked at him a moment.

"Are jellyfish a special interest of yours, Commander?"

"At the moment, yes."

"Well, in fact, we have had trouble with jellyfish. They tend to drift into the suction valves and clog the filters. They are so delicate! So fragile. I think of them as angels. They are a difficult creature to keep in captivity."

"We too have had problems with them. We were hoping you could help us."

"I had no idea you concerned yourselves with such matters at the Space Colony. I have always thought of you more in terms of those tiny cows and horses. And those delightful redwood forests."

"Yes," Jim said, "but recently jellyfish have become a concern. You know what I am talking about, Thor."

"I can assure you, my dear Commander, I can't even guess. You seem to attach great significance to…jellyfish. Why would they be more important than sea urchins or starfish?"

"You mean to stand here and tell me to my face that you know nothing of the manufacture of jellyfish weapons?"

Thor bellowed in delight. "There is something very funny about that! Jelly beings! Jellybeans!"

Thor squeezed Commander Stewart around the shoulders and said to her in a serious tone, "My dear Commander, I am a lover of nature, of biodiversity. I collect God's creatures to preserve them, study them, and appreciate their form and function. It is something of a personal indulgence. But it gives both me and those who work with me on this dead world very, very great pleasure. I would not presume to take on the role of creator. I certainly wouldn't use what little I know about life's treasures to create some sort of…what? A biological weapon?"

Jim turned sharply to Commander Stewart. "I don't believe we will learn much from this dialogue. In addition," he said, glancing at Thor's arm around Elizabeth's shoulder, "this man is not a friend, regardless of your past ties."

He saluted Commander Stewart and strode out of the aquarium.

The little party stared after him, washed in green light.

"Lizzie, what's gotten into your commander?" Thor asked. "For the life of me, I don't know what he was talking about. Am I the enemy?"

Elizabeth explained that the Space Colony had recently been plagued by the mysterious jellyfish, communication satellites and solar collectors now being clogged by their numbers, which seemed to be growing. To some of her advisors, including Commander Mann, it seemed that someone had intentionally created these "creatures" as weapons to obstruct the workings of the Space Colony. Who other than the Lunar Colonists had any motive to do that? Elizabeth admitted she wasn't entirely convinced that the motive would stand up to examination.

"Goodness!" Thor grunted. "We have our differences. The Lunars definitely have complaints. We work hard. We have very little say over much of what we do. We live poor lives considering the riches we export. But sabotage or rebellion? I think not."

Thor stared at them a moment.

"We depend on the Space Colony. You are a lifeline of supplies and information. And the Space Colony depends on us certainly—for raw materials, oxygen, water, and now that the fusion reactor is complete, energy. There can't be a revolution or civil war. We all know this. We are in this together. Any business breakdown would hurt us horribly."

"Someone has to explain those jellyfish," TF's father said. "Commander Mann didn't just make those up."

"Maybe it would be more profitable if we worked on the problem together," Thor said. "Do you have a specimen?"

"Amelia?" Commander Stewart asked. "Can you describe the jellyfish?"

"They're tiny," Amelia said. "About the size of quarters. You can almost see through them, just like jellyfish on Earth.

They are a beautiful blue color. But they can sting. Their stings feel like touching nettles."

"And they attack computers," TF chimed in. "They seem to be seeking information. One of them completely stripped an onboard computer of its programs. They are powered by a central processing unit of gallium arsenide, like the old computers."

"So they are manufactured," Thor said.

"And that means who but the Lunars?" TF's father said.

"Putting that nonsense aside," Thor said, "I will have to give this some thought. I will consult with staff. In the meantime, I have a gift for the children."

Thor led them to a large bed of sand and water and sea grass. It was about 60 feet long. It was like a section of beach Amelia used to know in Pacific Grove. A few small birds scurried back and forth as the water pulsed in and out, like waves. "They were raised from eggs," Thor explained. "They can walk but seem unable or unwilling to fly. Perhaps you would like to take them back to the Farm Zone."

Thor picked two birds up in his huge hands and gently placed one in Amelia's hands and one in TF's.

"This is a tern," Amelia said.

"It's your tern now!" Thor said and chortled.

Elizabeth groaned. "You're terrible," she said.

"Oh, Thorily," Thor punned again and roared with delight. Commander Mann's accusations didn't seem to dampen his spirits or humor.

"Such a huge man, such tiny jokes," TF whispered to Amelia.

CHAPTER 9

The community meeting that followed the tour of the aquarium was, as Commander Stewart had hoped, polite. It reminded Amelia very much of the community council meetings Gramps and Gran had dragged her to in Pacific Grove.

"People have trouble working together," Gramps had said. "I remember when I was shoeing horses, there was a joke that two horseshoers would argue about the color of a horse. Council meetings are worse. You learn patience."

The room filled up with several hundred gangly colonists. Amelia and TF had to sit in front just so that they could see. Even the kids were tall. It was like being in a room full of basketball players, who all wore their hair in long braids.

Commander Stewart, Commander Francis, Commander Mann, and Thor sat with microphones at a table in front of the room.

It was strange to see her father look so small next to Thor. He had, however, regained his composure and was being more diplomatic. After brief speeches from Elizabeth and Thor, the colonists presented their concerns. About two dozen of them spoke.

They were, as Thor had said, tired of working so hard and earning so little. They were tired of mining oxygen, water, iron, nickel and titanium and slinging ore into space with the mass driver without making a decent profit. They had risked their lives to supply the building materials and to build the Solar Power Satellites. Yet they had worked for little more than hourly wages. They had built the fusion reactor and mined the helium 3 to power it. Why weren't they seeing more profit? Why weren't their lives improving?

Commander Mann reminded them that they had medical care, free. They did not have to worry about retirement. The government paid for all this. Was it really so grim?

"No one retires on the moon," Thor pointed out. "There is too much work to do."

Members of the audience laughed. They had other gripes. Why did seats on the OTVs always get filled with travelers from the Space Colony instead of the Lunar Colony? They felt like second-class citizens. Perhaps, one speaker suggested, the big shots on Earth and at the Space Colony should visit the moon more often—and see what life was like here.

Commander Stewart apologized for not having visited more regularly. She urged the colonists to form a committee and make up a list of complaints and suggestions for solving them. There were, of course, officials already doing this but it was important to hear directly from the people.

Thor summarized. The Lunars were victims of history. The Space Colony was a great building. The Lunar settlement was the construction site and the shacks for the workers. Power and authority were established on the spinning wheel, and neither power nor authority likes to share. But change is necessary as the situation changes.

"Now, the Lunar Colony has a life of its own," Thor said. "We are no longer merely a construction site. This is our world. We can no longer go back to Earth and we don't want to."

Cheers.

"It is time for us take our rightful place," Thor continued. "As humans begin their next step into space—to Mars and beyond—it is the Lunars who will provide the island stepping-off point. After all, Lunars are better adapted to near weightless conditions. We should not, and will not, be treated like second-class citizens. Our destiny is the stars!"

The colonists cheered. Commander Stewart applauded. Amelia could see her father fighting off a frown, and then a messenger whispered something in his ear. He stiffened a little at whatever news had been delivered. He didn't say anything, and a hard look settled over his features.

It was only after the meeting that Amelia found out what was going on. She sat and TF kept quiet as the adults made their way from the meeting to their sleeping quarters.

They rode on a transporter belt, huddled in a group. At a little distance, Lunar Colony guards stood, with their arms crossed.

"They've interrupted ore shipments," Jim hissed to Elizabeth. "Oxygen and water shipments are also breaking down. While we listened to their complaints, they were cutting the Space Colony off from vital resources. I've put all systems on alert."

"Are the reports complete?" Commander Stewart asked.

"No," Jim said. "We only know that two shipments have definitely been blocked. We have asked for an explanation from the Lunar systems."

Elizabeth summed up, "At the moment, no other action is required."

"Some other action might be desirable, however," Jim said. "Isn't it obvious that your friend isn't telling the truth?"

"No, Jim," Elizabeth replied crisply. "That is not entirely obvious. Be a little more patient."

"Patience is not always a virtue," Jim said.

"It is always useful," Elizabeth said.

Amelia smoothed the feathers of the tern she still held in her hands.

Back in their quarters, Amelia and TF compared notes.

"It's weird," TF said. "We know more about those jellyfish than the bigwigs. Because they always go in looking using the TAS. I think we're right. The jellyfish avoid that system."

"Why?" Amelia asked. She lay above TF in a bunk bed. It was nice to be in a bed again, even if gravity was only a sixth of Earth's. Their compartment had been darkened, but outside she knew it was light. There were still several more days— 24 hour periods—to the lunar day.

"TAS has too much security for the jellyfish." TF said. "When they attacked your system, you weren't on TAS. Neither of us were. Doesn't that make sense?"

"I agree with Commander Stewart," Amelia said. "Thor doesn't know anything about them."

TF said, "Our fathers are wrong."

"But I don't see what we can do about it," Amelia said. "We *are* just kids. If we could only get a good look at one of those jellyfish. There must be a program. We could decode it. That would tell us *who, what, when,* and *where.*"

"And *why*?"

"Where! Where! That's the question," Amelia snapped. "Where is the Queen Bee?"

"We have to get into Dad's lab. Nothing's security-blocked there," replied TF.

The next "day" on the moon was one long field trip. Thor thought it was important for the Space Colony officials to get a first-hand look at what was going on at the fusion reactor, the mines, and the mass driver. "Look at our toys," he half joked with the group.

A Lunar Transport Vehicle carried the party from site to site. It was like a huge tank, with treads of steel. Thor acted as their tour guide. He geared his talk to the reporters who tagged along. Amelia already knew a lot of what he said. She was sure her father already knew all this. But Thor's voice made it seem important and new. Maybe he *was* a bit of a showman.

"Perhaps most important to our future economy is the fusion reactor. This is the first time humans have successfully recreated the process that powers the stars, including our own sun. Instead of splitting atoms, we join or fuse them. This requires enormous heat. The trick is to generate core temperatures of 200 million degrees on a small, efficient, and controllable scale. Otherwise, we would have a reaction going that could annihilate the entire moon and maybe the Earth. We have created a *tiny* sun. But even tiny suns can be the stuff of nightmares," he added softly.

"What is remarkable about the moon," Thor continued, in a brisk tour-guide way, "is the amount of a substance that is fairly rare on Earth—helium 3. This molecule is generated by the sun and sprayed into space on the solar wind. This stardust has been falling on the moon's surface for 4 billion years. It is much less radioactive than other fuels used for fusion. There is enough helium 3 on the moon to meet Earth's energy needs for thousands of years. It may be the moon's most valuable export."

Thor took the group from the fusion reactor to one of the

many mass drivers located on the moon's surface. The mass driver was a tube nearly a mile long that accelerated buckets of ore—iron, nickel and titanium—from zero to several hundred miles an hour in a second. It did this by giving the ore load little magnetic pushes as the bucket accelerated along the tube.

"The old Norse god Thor would hurl his hammer," Thor said. "This is my version. It is really as simple, basically, as a hammer or a slingshot reaction. Of course, the mass driver can also be used as an engine. Every action has an equal and opposite action. By spitting out something, the mass driver can create a force movement in the opposite direction, like the old jet engines. A mass driver was used, for example, to move Phoebe to its present position. The asteroid itself provided the fuel."

Thor went on: "After being fired into space, the ore is collected and transferred to a Lunar Ore Carrier, processed at the Space Colony, and then put into a low Earth orbit. The finished product is then collected by robots and brought down to Earth, which, as you know, is now starved for certain minerals. We're earning our way on this one."

"Isn't the flow supposed to be continuous?" Jim asked.

"Yes," Thor said. "A continuous flow is the most efficient."

"How do you explain the fact that within the last 24 hours both shipments of ore and oxygen have been interrupted?"

"I cannot explain that," Thor said.

"I find that difficult to believe," Jim said.

Thor said. "Excuse me a moment." He spoke into his communicator and a voice crackled back. Yes, shipments had been interrupted due to interference with communication satellites in the L5 orbit. Lunar Colonists had been in contact with the Space Colonists about this.

"It would appear, Commander, that the problem is at your end," Thor said. "Our ships can't navigate without functioning communication satellites."

Commander Mann's tone was ice-cold. "And you claim to know nothing about the jellyfish that are fouling the satellites?"

"Only what I have learned in the last few hours," Thor said. "I understand your concern, and I have expressed my willingness to help in any way I can."

Jim glanced at the reporters, who had huddled close, their recorders held high. "You might consider calling them off," he said and then calmly turned to Commander Stewart.

"The situation could go critical in the next 15 hours. I suggest that our presence will be required back home," he said to Elizabeth.

Her father sounded strange, Amelia thought. He sounded like someone in a war game, so cool, so efficient, so ready to blow up a world.

In any case, they cut their moon trip short and left for the Space Colony. Cap and her father and Commander Stewart talked among themselves in hushed tones for nearly the entire ten-hour trip. TF and Amelia sat with their new birds in tiny cages in their laps.

They played chess again. Amelia became more aggressive in her mid-game and even succeeded in getting a draw from TF. Chess was a complicated game, but it was a lot simpler than life.

"I've got one," TF said to Amelia over the communicator. "I'm in the lab."

It had become dismally clear to Amelia that TF was a morning person. She, on the other hand, liked starting slowly. She still needed time to recover from the long trip back from the moon.

"TF, it's only five in the morning," Amelia complained. "We just got home last night."

"The early bird gets the worm," TF said. "I've been out in the MMU this morning and I've got one trapped."

TF clicked off, and Amelia reluctantly crawled out of her sleeping bag. TF was more excited than she had ever heard him. Where did he get all that energy? Was this not sleeping part of his plan to live on the moon where a day was two weeks long? She floated in her cell and caught herself falling asleep.

She climbed into the "washing machine." She was almost used to this contraption, but it would never be as satisfying as a real shower on Earth. She looked forward to moving to the Farm Zone, where people took real showers. She wondered what her father had meant by saying that these quarters were just temporary and that he and Amelia would be moving to the Farm Zone if all went as planned. She had meant to ask him about the plan.

When she emerged from the shower, there was another message from TF on her message recorder. "I know where they come from. I know how they work. I can control them. I really need some help."

Amelia yawned and sighed. Washed and air-dried, Amelia put on her overalls, brushed her hair (not so easy in nil gravity) and headed to the hub.

When she got to the lab, she saw TF tumbling about, flicking himself from screen to screen. "I've got my hands full," he said.

Amelia saw that the jellyfish was enclosed in thick glass, the heat-resistant stuff made on the moon for rockets and buildings. Inside, the jellyfish had attached itself to a small box TF had designed, just as the jellyfish had attached itself to Amelia's MMU computer console. A heavy cable ran from the box to a computer outside the aquarium.

TF explained, "I gave it some software to attack. That same software should record what's going on in the jellyfish. If this works, we're going to see what makes this thing tick."

One of the laser printers slid out a long thin strip of paper. TF snatched at it and then groaned.

"I knew it," he said desperately to Amelia. "This is way beyond me. It's like I can only read every tenth word. This'll take hours."

Other printers started extruding paper, thick, wide sheets, skinny strips, and everything in between. Soon the air was a blizzard of floating printouts.

"Faffle! And double faffle!" TF snapped to no one in particular, panic in his eyes.

"Moderato cantabile," Amelia said singingly, and grinned. Then she directed briskly.

"Take all the sheets and pin them up on that wall. Then you can see the whole game. Then you can move the pieces around."

"Right," TF chirped and did exactly as he was told.

"In the meantime," TF said, "you have to do the history. Something here is making these things, not the moon. The only possible place is Phoebe, the old garbage dump. It was shut down long before Commander Stewart and your father were appointed. Find out about Phoebe!"

TF directed Amelia to a console and told her it was the one her father used. He fiddled with the keyboard a moment and ducked his head sheepishly.

"I'll bet I know his password. It's one of three names." His fingers danced across the keyboard once, twice, and then three times.

"Yup. It's here. The code word was Margaret, your mother's name, right? Now you have complete access, no security blocks. Find us a bad guy."

Amelia fastened herself at the console with Velcro straps and called up Phoebe. She was appalled. The menu had thousands of entries. There were a hundreds even under History. She called up a few entries at random and got long, formal reports, full of mysterious equations and extremely long words.

"Faffle!" she thought. "I'll never understand this gobbledy-gook. I'm just a kid."

And that gave her a great idea.

She scrolled for entries with a *J* in them—for "Juvenile." After all, if you wanted to find something explained simply, look at stuff written for kids!

She skimmed feverishly. Gradually an overall picture formed—general information about Phoebe as a dump today. What about long ago? Amelia looked for the oldest date she could find and called up 2017. There she found her second clue, in a picture book for tots. She saw a painting of a long row of old-fashioned mainframe computers. The text said: "This is a small part of the computer that runs the asteroid called Phoebe. The computer is called Diana.

Bingo!

Amelia called up Diana. Here, too, were thousands of entries. But by using her J approach and looking for old titles, she quickly had the main outlines. In her time, Diana was the largest and "smartest" computer in space.

The only problem was that Diana had been shut down! Now she was just a dumb minicomputer, with just enough smarts and power to check visitors and keep the lights on. Surely her father knew all this? There was only way to be sure.

With a deep sense of dread—and of doing something so wrong it amounted to evil—she called up her father's Personal Log.

Although she scrolled it quickly, trying not to read, she gasped at the pain hidden in the cold green letters.

"Amelia?" TF called out.

"Stay away, TF!" Amelia almost screamed. No one else was going to see this, ever.

On a hunch, Amelia checked a date she knew all too well, the day of the Scramjet crash.

The screen filled with columns of figures and graphs. But there at the bottom was a note in English. "Diana seems to be running a teensy fever. Check out. Tomorrow is the great day!"

Amelia did a global search, but found no later reference to Diana.

As she scanned, she couldn't help picking out bits of torment. That her father blamed himself for Mom's death. And for crippling his daughter! He was terrified Amelia would hate Elizabeth. Would he lose Elizabeth? Could he hurt his only child so badly, once again? Amelia saw in the entries the tracks of a man growing sour and bitter and half-mad with hurt.

Dry-eyed, she shut down and stared into the middle distance.

"I've got it," she said tonelessly.

"Faffle! I don't!" TF screeched. "Bits and pieces is all."

He rattled off what he had. It didn't look good for the Lunars, in fact. The chip in the jellyfish was arsenide, used on the moon a generation ago. The "stinger" was a miniature laser, combined with an optical sensor, also once used by moon robots. The creatures had a huge memory. TF couldn't be sure, but it looked as if they were programmed to transmit data and somehow reproduce when they were half-full of it. But transmit where? To whom? Maybe they could be stopped by decoys, like his. Maybe they could be fed sterile data, sort of like the way farmers controlled insect pests.

"It's Diana," Amelia said, still staring.

"Who?" TF asked.

"Diana, the computer who runs Phoebe."

"But that's been shut down for 25 years!"

Amelia unstrapped herself and pushed off. She floated near the ceiling and looked down at TF as though from a great distance.

She explained. "You're alive. You are infinitely clever. You have actually designed most of the Lunar and Space Colonies. Your robots have done much of the work. You are called Diana, and you are programmed to protect and nurture your nests and all who live in them. You are programmed to survive, in order to serve.

"Then you are unplugged, left only with a few brain cells out of trillions. What would you do, TF?"

TF stared at her. There was something different about her face, as though she was no longer a little girl.

"It's impossible." TF shook his head. "Somebody would have noticed, checked."

"My father did. He called it a 'teensy fever' and made a note to look into it. It was the day Mom was killed. He never went back to it."

TF clapped his forehead. "And even if he did, Diana had had her first drones out. She'd be clever enough to cook the readouts after that!"

A message boomed out from TF's communicator. "THOMAS FRANCIS. YOU ARE REQUIRED TO REPORT TO SECURITY IMMEDIATELY. REPEAT: IMMEDIATELY. THIS IS PRIORITY RED.

"Uh-oh. This will be taken out of our hands anyway," TF said. "We have to respond."

Amelia and TF whooshed out of the hub, picked up Amelia's wheelchair, and then whooshed to the Rim, where Security had its headquarters. Two guards met them and escorted them into a office where TF's father and a Security officer waited.

"TF," his father said, "Where have you been?"

"Collecting," TF said. "Then the lab."

"Collecting what?"

"A jellyfish."

"You have one?"

"Yes, sir. It is contained. In your lab."

"TF, we received a report from the Space Cadets just minutes ago. From a monitored communication, they said you told Amelia, 'I can control them.' I presume this relates to the jellyfish."

"Yes, sir."

"I hope you intended to notify us eventually. You know that Commanders Stewart and Mann are both contemplating some sort of defensive action. Do you have other information you aren't sharing with us?"

TF said earnestly, his voice squeaking only a little, "No, sir. They come from Phoebe. Diana is making them. I have some ideas for dealing with them."

Cap sighed deeply and pinched his eyes, as though he had a headache. "TF, I never thought I'd hear you talk non-sense. These jellyfish aren't some project of yours that got out of hand?"

TF shook his head vigorously. "No, sir."

"Security is concerned. You are up to your eyeballs in a classified matter," his father said warily. "They have asked that you be confined to the Farm Zone. They want to do an investigation."

"I'm just a kid!" TF said. Despite herself, Amelia giggled. She just couldn't help it. Then, she said in her firmest voice, "It's true. Everything he's said is true."

"You are, in a sense, a prime 'suspect.'" Cap continued,

ignoring Amelia.

"That's crazy!" TF said, with great indignation.

"You do have a track record," the security chief, Colonel Smith, reminded TF. He was a small, bright-looking man with a slight twitch in one eyebrow. He tapped a file with TF's name on it. "You are the only eleven-year-old in the Space Colony with his own Security file. Remember those rodents, the voles you somehow bred into the Farm Zone that just about destroyed a habitat? Or the virus you somehow got into TAS? Or…I won't go into your dismal record of fouling things up."

TF looked a little sheepish. "Voles. There was a temporary imbalance. But a few snakes solved the problem. It was an ecological experiment."

TF's father banged the desk angrily. "Your experiments aren't always as controlled as one would like. And these jelly-fish have the earmark of your tinkering. Couldn't you be just a little more like the Space Cadets? They are *nice* kids. They seem to stay out of trouble."

"I wish the Space Cadets would mind their own business," TF said.

"They are empowered to monitor the Station's young people. You know that. In any case, that is not the point."

"So am I arrested? In the name of freedom?"

"Security has asked that you be temporarily restricted to the Farm Zone," Cap said. "That means not using MMUs or conducting further experiments in the lab. This is only temporary. It wouldn't be proper for you to receive special treatment because you are my son or because Amelia is the Commander's daughter."

"Is Amelia arrested, too?"

"No one has been arrested. We're requesting that you both stop messing around for a few days, until we get things sorted out. We simply can't afford to spend any more time on you two. Not during this crisis. Maybe you could work up some duets. You both play beautifully."

"Thank you," Amelia said. "Will you tell my father what we have found?"

TF said nothing and stuck out his lower lip.

"Commander Mann is in a Priority Red Council with Commander Stewart. I'm due there myself just about now," TF's father said as he checked his communicator.

The head of Security observed drily, "Commander Stewart will be notified of the results of this meeting and a complete transcript will of course be attached to your file. And to yours, young lady." He twitched at Amelia.

"And Diana has been kaput for 25 years," Cap said flatly. "I checked the readouts last week. She's as dead as a doornail."

"Diana is smarter than all of us!" Amelia protested. "Including Security," she added defiantly.

"That will be all, Amelia," said her father. "Security is just doing its job."

TF stuck his lip back out.

"Just take it easy for a day or two," TF's father said. "Amelia, will you please keep an eye on this young fellow?"

Amelia shrugged. "Not easy," she said.

"Oh, I know, I know," Cap said.

That evening, Amelia and TF watched the news over a dinner of barley and tomato soup, warm and secure in the comfort of TF's home. Outside, the situation was not secure or comfortable.

There was close-up footage of the jellyfish, hanging like monarch butterflies on the communication satellites. There were thousands of them. A newscaster reported: "Words have been exchanged between officials of the Space Colony and the Lunar Colony. Commander Stewart has said that the Space Colony is considering a variety of options. On Earth, unidentified military officials have rated the situation as critical. Meanwhile, oxygen and water supplies on the Space Colony are being carefully monitored."

Commander Stewart appeared on the screen and spoke in her calming way. "Our scientists have determined that these jellyfish are actually manufactured. We are not yet sure who has created them or why. I would like to emphasize that we have no indications that the Lunar Colonists are in any way responsible for this invasion of our communications. In fact, they have expressed their willingness to help in any way possible. Several options for dealing with the situation are being considered, and the administration has made the situation a Red Priority, of course."

"What they don't say," TF said, "is that the whole fleet of

laser interceptors have been put on 24-hour alert. Who do you think they'll go after? Not jellyfish. Also the mass drivers on the moon have been redirected. If push comes to shove, they can be used as catapults. It's kind of primitive, but it works. The Lunar Colonists could throw a bunch of rocks at us. It's funny how grown-ups let things get blown up so quickly. I mean, they were actually given the answer!

"We might do some good if we could get to Phoebe," TF added.

"We were just told not to leave the Farm Zone," Amelia pointed out.

"It could be that we don't have to physically go to Phoebe. We'd just have to figure out something remote. You saw the access codes on the printout? I need those printouts. This will require some thought. I might have to get into the lab just one more time."

Amelia could see that TF was indeed thinking. His moon face was blank, and his lips were pursed, as though around a lollipop.

CHAPTER 11

A rooster crowed. The horses whinnied and nickered in their stalls, and the cows lowed as they plodded in a line to pasture. Amelia awoke early to the unfamiliar sounds and in an unfamiliar bed, the first time she had slept with full gravity since leaving Earth. She felt stiff. It took her a moment to figure out where she was—at TF's house in the Farm Zone. TF was already up and doing the exercises he did every day.

TF's mother, Lillian, was also up and brewing tea. "How are the juvenile delinquents this morning?" she asked when Amelia and TF joined her in the kitchen.

"I guess you mean those big children who are rattling their swords—or laser guns—at each other and calling each other names?" said TF.

Lillian laughed. "It's a little like the old Earth game of Mutually Assured Destruction, MAD. In the old days, the super powers would point their missiles at each other. And their strategy was 'We'll all go down together.'"

"A century later, the same thing's going on," Amelia said.

"Slow learners," TF commented. "The Lunar Colonists aren't even enemies."

"What is it about people?" Amelia asked. "How could good people like our fathers and Thor risk everything?"

"It's been a question about human psychology for hundreds of years," Lillian said. "Our technical progress doesn't seem to have had any effect on the primitive, violent part of human nature."

"We still have a lot of the same genetic structure as a chimpanzee." TF said. "In effect, we still have a lot of the programming that helped us hunt and fight off predators 2 million years ago. We're a bunch of animals when you scratch the surface. Any animal will get nasty when faced with extinction."

"Except chimpanzees don't have mass drivers and fusion reactors and laser canons," Amelia said.

"I wouldn't worry too much," Lillian comforted. "They'll come to their senses. Commander Stewart is a reasonable person. She and Thor have been friends for a long time. I believe they're meeting this afternoon. I know Jim and Cap will be gone."

"Maybe the moon really does cause insanity," TF said. "They're sure acting like a bunch of lunatics. Who ever heard of arresting eleven-year-olds?"

TF's feelings were still bruised. He had thought that truth always won immediately.

Lillian pointed out that the astronomer Galileo had been arrested for suggesting that Earth was not the center of the solar system. "Sometimes, it takes a little time for the truth to take hold. Even if you're right, you have to have patience."

"But it's so boring!" TF exclaimed. "People do the same thing over and over!"

"This is getting too philosophical for me," Lillian said. "I think I need to do some gardening."

According to the morning news, the Space Colony was now operating on reserve supplies of oxygen. Unless shipments were resumed, those supplies could be exhausted in a week's time. Evacuation plans were being reviewed and prepared. There would be a special meeting with the Lunar Colonists later in the afternoon, on a ship half way between the moon and L5.

"I need to visit the lab one more time," TF said.

"We'll get into huge trouble," Amelia said.

"It may be worth it," TF said.

"Do you think we can use the jellyfish to get at Diana?"

"That's the plan," TF said. "I'm pretty sure the access codes are all contained in its programming. This is going to require a bit of…a plan."

"I figured," Amelia said.

"Amelia and I have decided to work on our music today," TF announced to his mother.

TF's plan was to practice together for an hour and tape the session. "When we're done, we just put the machine on repeat and we're out of here. My mother won't interrupt us if it sounds like we're working."

"Hmph," Amelia said, not quite sure. "TF, you have a truly deceitful nature!"

"Well, didn't you ever do it? Weren't there times you just didn't feel like practicing?"

"Actually," Amelia said, "no one ever made me practice. Even when it was hard and boring, I sort of loved it."

"I always wanted to play the accordion, but my parents wouldn't let me," TF said. "They said it wasn't really a musical instrument."

"I would tend to agree with them," Amelia teased.

"You're a snob," TF retorted, only half teasing.

After an hour of playing and taping, Amelia and TF snuck out of the cabin and left the Farm Zone, using a tunnel that TF didn't think would be watched, rather than the Whoosh. "This system of tunnels was designed as a shelter system," TF explained. "It was supposed to let people get around when the radiation shields weren't functioning properly, which happened a lot in the early days. They're still used during solar storms. I used to play here," he added. "I think I can get us to the hub."

He walked as Amelia rolled and then floated through the narrow dark tunnels. It took them almost an hour to get to the hub.

"So far, so good," TF said as they emerged into the long hallway leading to the zero-gravity labs. Very quietly, they made their way closer.

Their luck had run out. Two uniformed Security guards, playing cards, lounged just outside the lab. "They don't trust us!" TF said in disgust.

"Well, they were right," Amelia commented. "Your mother trusted us, and look what we did to her. I feel guilty."

"But still, don't you think that's a little insulting?"

"TF, you're being silly."

"In any case, we have a problem."

"Yes," Amelia agreed. "Maybe I could distract them long enough for you to do your dirty work."

"How?"

"The renegade wheelchair might do the trick. Ready to roll?"

TF nodded.

"Here goes," Amelia said. She took a deep breath. She adjusted its controls, revving up the motor. "Cruise control," she said and let it rip. The chair took off down the hallway toward the guards. She pushed off the wall in hot pursuit. The chair accelerated and bounced off the walls. The startled guards had to duck just to miss being hit. Amelia screamed for help and nearly crashed into the guards as she herself rebounded off the walls, pushing, getting up more speed as she somersaulted after her chair.

As she hoped, the guards pushed off after her. She had a head start and was 50 yards down the hallway and around a bend before they could reach her. "My chair! My chair!" she cried. They took off down the hallway, leaving her behind. Maybe TF was right, she thought. These Security people were kind and helpful but not too swift.

Eventually the two guards returned, chair in hand.

"Oh, thank you!" Amelia said. "It just got away from me. I don't know what I would have done without your help."

"You have to be careful," one of the guards said, breathing heavily. "Zero gravity is tricky if you're not used to it."

"Yes, it's very tricky," Amelia said. "I'll have to be more careful." She proceeded very slowly back along the hallway, talking to the guards. At the door to the lab, she thanked them again and helped them gather their cards, which were floating all over the hallway.

Around the corner of the hallway, she found TF fuming.

"Did you get it?" she asked.

"It's gone."

"Gone?"

"The jellyfish. It's the only specimen they've got."

"Why were they guarding the lab then?"

"Who knows? I got the printouts though."

A special bulletin was broadcast over a hall screen. Space Colony officials had issued an ultimatum to Lunar Colonists. The mass driver must be reoriented within two hours to avoid the risk of a military strike. The Colony's interceptor ships had been placed on full alert and readiness. Reinforcements were being sent from Earth.

"This is getting out of hand," TF said.

"This is incredible!" Amelia cried. "They're actually talking war! Over a bunch of jellyfish."

"It's time for a Children's Crusade," TF said mysteriously. "We've got to move fast. To Phoebe."

"Uh-oh," said Amelia dubiously.

TF waved the printouts at her. "Maybe, just maybe, I can turn Diana off. You have a better idea?"

TF led the way to a small docking port. A guard politely issued them P-suits and filled out an authorization form. Still packing Amelia's wheelchair, they scrambled into the pressure suits, piled into an MMU, and blasted off in a matter of minutes, just as blue-alert lights began flashing around them.

"That was too easy," TF commented as he adjusted the thrusters. "So much for Security. But they'll be after us, when the Space Weenies—I mean Space Cadets—spot us."

12

CHAPTER

The MMU with Amelia and TF zipped past the communication satellites and the factory modules. "We'll see just how fast this baby can boogie," TF said. Amelia felt the G-forces press her back into her seat. Their communicators crackled with the same messages that came over the intercom: URGENT: MMU NUMBER *766* RETURN TO HUB. FLIGHT PLAN DENIED. RETURN TO HUB.

"MMU *766* unable to respond," TF said back to the communicator. "Will oblige as soon as possible."

TF scanned the web as the red-alert lights went on and zipped through a hole. "See if you can call up a map of Phoebe," he said to Amelia. "We'll need a docking port on the far side, if there is one. There won't be anyone there. After all, Phoebe is in the line of fire if the Lunies start heaving rocks."

"Should we hook into TAS?" Amelia asked.

"No!" TF barked. "We need to keep a low profile."

Amelia typed in a few commands. "Here it is," Amelia said. A map of Phoebe appeared on the computer screen. It was a maze of tunnels and storage caves. Amelia found a small auxiliary port.

"Can you find a terminal anywhere?" TF asked. "We've got to say things to Diana."

Amelia squinted at the bright green display, then pointed. "There! Right there! Close to the docking port." TF leaned over to look.

"Maybe our luck is shifting. We'll need every second. Any sign of pursuit?"

Amelia glanced at the scanner. "No. So far, we're free and clear. Is there any chance this is going to work?" she asked.

"It depends. If Diana has revised her security codes, forget it. If not, it will be a piece of cake. Those codes are all old news. And they weren't very tight to begin with. But then I have to speak Diana's language, which I'm not sure about. At all," TF emphasized.

TF docked quickly and quietly. The two of them pushed out of the capsule and floated into a port filled with flashing blue light. TF grabbed the laser blaster from the cabin, and Amelia strapped herself into her wheelchair, even though there was no gravity. "The thrusters might help," she said.

"UNAUTHORIZED PERSONNEL ON PREMISES," an

infinitely kind voice said over the speaker system. "RETURN TO THE DOCKING PORT IMMEDIATELY, PLEASE. ESCORT HAS BEEN REQUESTED."

But that wasn't the direction TF and Amelia were taking. They flew into a dimly lit hallway and then toward the large cave where the computer terminal had appeared on the map.

"Diana wouldn't have upgraded her escorts," TF said. "They'll be about as smart as human Security. But we still only have minutes to figure this thing out."

Diana's motherly voice spoke to them again. LEVEL ONE SECURITY BREACH. PLEASE RESPOND. I WILL RESORT TO GELETOX.

TF ignored Diana's warning and jabbed at the button outside the cave, and the sliding door hissed open like an elevator door.

TF gasped. The cave was empty! TF and Amelia searched the shadows. The stone here had been chiseled by laser drills. The surface was chipped away like the surface of an arrowhead. The pale light glinted off the dark rock.

"This place should be full of stuff!" TF said and his voice echoed, "Stuff, stuff, stuff…"

"Do you have the map?" He was frantic, and the printout shook as he held it. An incredible maze of tunnels and caves spread throughout the asteroid. There were other terminals marked there. But would any others still exist? Or had they all been decommissioned and removed?

He raced out of the cave in one leap and back into the

hallway. "Let's go!"

"Go! Go! Go!…," echoed the cave.

Amelia pushed after TF as he punched another door open only to reveal another empty, cold cave. Diana's voice again warned them to return to the docking port. Flashing blue and red lights created weird, moving shadows everywhere. A siren began to wail through the hallways.

Suddenly a robot about three feet high appeared behind them in the doorway. It sprayed multiple strands of plasticlike goo into the room, completely missing the two of them in the huge space.

"Let me cancel this canned nuisance," TF said.

One blast from TF's blaster sent the robot careening in small circles. However, another robot was right behind, spraying the same sticky strands. TF fired again with the same results.

"LEVEL 2 SECURITY BREACH," Diana's voice intoned, still kind. "PLEASE RESPOND. I WILL HAVE TO RESORT TO PENETRATING GAS."

"It's time for decoys," Amelia announced. "We'll give them two targets. You keep looking. I'll deal with the robots."

Without waiting for a response, Amelia fired up her wheelchair and took off down a dark hallway. A troop of midget robots buzzed after her, spraying gas and goo. They weren't used to anything traveling as fast as her wheelchair, Amelia thought, as she zigged and zagged through the ancient rock tunnels. She wondered if she would ever be able to find her way back.

She let one group of pursuing robots spray another group set up as a kind of roadblock. She simply cut to the right just as they fired. The strands of sticky goo were as hard on the robots as they would have been on her.

Diana was not pleased.

Diana's motherly voice was everywhere but the message it relayed was not comforting. "I AM AT LEVEL RED SECURITY BREACH. LASERS ARE AT FULL POWER. THEY WILL DESTROY HUMAN TISSUE. REPEAT. I AM NOW PREPARED TO USE LETHAL FORCE.

"Goodness," Amelia said out loud as she somersaulted to avoid a thin line of ruby-red death ray. "They're serious." She suckered several robots into a large empty cave, hanging above the entrance as they buzzed in. She dropped down behind them and zipped out, politely shutting the door behind her.

"Now, to find TF!" she said to herself, hoping he'd found a terminal. He called to her over the communicator.

"I found it!" he cried. "Can you get back? Need help!"

Amelia locked into TF's signal. She ripped through the hallways back to yet another huge cave. This one was furnished with computers and glowing green terminals.

Amelia punched the door shut behind her.

"Here she is—Diana!" TF exclaimed, already seated at a keyboard. Typing in a series of codes, he explained. "I got these from the downloading of the jellyfish. If the jellyfish can use them to access the computer, so can we."

He added mysteriously, "We have to go from *fish* to *fowl*, from *hate* to *love*, and from *cold* to *warm*."

"What are you talking about?" Amelia said.

The codes were basically word transforms, TF explained. First, the operator has to know the three word changes. Then, by changing only one letter at a time, the operator has to proceed through a series of English words from one word like FISH to FOWL.

"Watch," TF said. "It's just a word game." TF typed in the word FISH. "We change one letter to get…let's see…: FIST. Then we change another letter to get FAST. From there, we can go to FACT."

"FOWL is still a long way off," Amelia noted.

The computerized voice echoed in the cave, over the loudspeaker: "UNAUTHORIZED PERSONNEL MUST RETURN TO DOCKING PORT. SECURITY ESCORT IS *EN ROUTE*. REINFORCEMENTS HAVE BEEN SUMMONED FROM L5."

TF typed furiously: FACE, FARE, CARE, CARS, CAWS.

"Is CAWS a word?" Amelia asked.

"The crow caws," TF said.

He continued typing: COWS, BOWS, BOWL, and finally the word FOWL.

"That might not be the simplest solution," TF said. "But maybe it will work."

Precious seconds ticked away as the sequence of words hovered on the screen. "FISH to FOWL confirmed" flashed across the bottom of the screen.

"Great!" TF said. "Two more."

The computer opened up another screen and TF typed in the transform: HATE to LOVE.

"You want to try this one?" he asked. "I'm a little wired."

Amelia sat down and typed in the word HAVE. Then RAVE, ROVE, and LOVE.

"Great! Very nice," TF said. "One more and we're in."

COLD to WARM. Amelia worked quickly: CORD, WORD, WARD, WARM.

"We're in!" TF shrieked.

A map of computer files opened.

"SECURITY REINFORCEMENTS PREPARING TO DOCK," the loudspeaker announced. "UNAUTHORIZED PERSONNEL MUST RETURN TO DOCKING PORT."

"I'm glad I closed that door," Amelia said as a robot fired laser beams outside and the thick steel sizzled with the heat.

"Now we have to guess what Diana calls her jellyfish," TF said, frantically scrolling through the menus. "Faffle! She has hundreds of files!"

TF scanned the library for commands he could use. "Come on, come on!" he said as he scrolled down the commands.

"Anything under Babies?" Amelia asked. "Chicks?"

"No."

"Children?"

"No."

"Helpers?"

"No."

"Kids?"

"No."

"Offspring?"

"No."

"I can't think of anything else," Amelia wailed.

"Progeny," TF said calmly. "What does that mean?"

"That's it!" Amelia cried.

TF called up the file and chose RETRIEVE from the menu. Then, just to be sure, he typed in another command, ABORT. REPEAT: RETRIEVE AND ABORT

"That's all I can think to do," he said. "Let's hope the result is instantaneous. Let's get out of here. I don't want to be here if the Lunies let loose."

Firing a laser blast at the robot in the doorway, they left the cave and hurried back down the hallway. Lights still flashed blue and red, and the loudspeakers continued to demand their return to the docking port. "We're coming, we're coming!" TF said. "And let's hope Security went in the front door!"

They scrambled back into the MMU and hooked into TAS just as a Security ship eased into the main airlock. "How's that for timing?" TF asked.

"I'm impressed," Amelia said. TAS was alive with information. All the monitors were already reporting that jelly-fish seemed to be letting go and then mysteriously dissipating, losing their form.

"It's working!" Amelia cried.

TF asked. "Is there any video news?"

Amelia scanned the channels. There were long clips of the mass drivers, ominously aimed at the Space Station. There were shots of a fleet of laser interceptors on their way from Earth. There was a report that officials from the Space Colony had joined with Lunar Colonists for a last-ditch effort to settle the matter peacefully.

"No baseball?" TF joked. They could relax a little.

TF was maneuvering the MMU through the web. "Boy, it's tight today. They've got it at full force. Here we go—a nick in the armor."

He zipped back through the web of microwave sensors. He noted that he was being trailed by two laser interceptors. But they seemed to be following at a respectful distance.

The Space Colony's own security fleet hovered in formation on the video screen.

"Well, at least they're not blasting away yet. Maybe we made it in time."

A moment later, Thor suddenly appeared on the screen, surrounded by a crowd of reporters. Commander Mann stood behind him on the left. Commander Stewart was on his right.

"Yes, we have news," Thor was saying. "And it is good news. Communication satellites have apparently been freed of encumbrances. Our ships should be able to navigate and to resume shipments within the next few hours. I believe the potential for hostilities no longer exists. Is that right, Commander?"

Commander Stewart stepped up to the microphone. "An unfortunate misunderstanding has been resolved. Although several questions remain to be answered, there seems to be no immediate danger. Space Colony forces have been relieved from Red status. Lunar Commander Thor has instructed the mass drivers to be reoriented. In addition, transport ships will be functioning again in a matter of hours."

"We did it," TF said softly. "Mission complete. How was that for an action-packed end game?"

He docked the MMU, and they floated into the hub. "We'd better get back to practicing," he said. "If we're lucky, Mother will have been gardening through all this. That's how she copes with stress. We certainly don't need to get into any more trouble."

"I've been thinking," Amelia said. "Those jellyfish were listed as 'progeny.' That means that Diana thought of them as her babies after all."

"They're talking about towing the whole asteroid out to space."

"That seems like a terrible waste."

"It won't be the first time Space wastes things."

"I wonder if my father has really thought about this," Amelia said.

"He's the expert," TF said.

"Yeah, but…." Her eyes filled. "But he hasn't been thinking too clearly. Maybe there's something he's missing."

"Like what?"

"Well, isn't the mission to Mars suffering from budget cuts? Aren't there all sorts of arguments about sending humans that far out? Here we have a giant computer who's done it all before. Couldn't they drag Phoebe to Mars and have computer-produced robots do the groundwork?"

"Faffle and double faffle on these experts!" TF said angrily, and this time his voice didn't screech. It came out as a pleasant baritone!

TF looked as surprised as a large puppy who's learned to bark and is astonished to find it is a loud, deep bark.

TF laughed. "We'll tell 'em to recycle Phoebe and Diana. But we'll have some explaining to do before we have too much credibility. Bet on it."

Back in the Farm Zone, they managed to reenter the house unnoticed, take up their instruments, and sight-read two thirds of a Beethoven piano trio. In an expansive mood, they gave the piano part to TAS.

"Hey!" Amelia said, "this isn't too bad! We've found ourselves a pianist."

"Even TAS has its uses," TF murmured.

"Doesn't play with much feeling," Amelia said.

"Well, I don't know about you," TF said, "but I've had just about enough feeling for one day."

As the TAS computer struggled during the second movement to fit the piano part into the live music of the two kids, Amelia found herself thinking about Diana. After they punched in the commands, Amelia thought she had heard something. It sounded for all the world like a sad sigh, like a mother giving up.

Now her own eyes filled until she could no longer see out of them.

EPILOGUE

Commander Stewart, Commander Mann, and TF's father returned, hailed as heroes, surrounded by reporters.

Commander Mann looked exhausted but relaxed. When he spotted Amelia, he floated away from the reporters, plucked her from her chair, and hugged her.

"I'm so glad you're safe!" he said.

"I'm so glad we're all safe," she answered. "The Lunar Colonists and all of us here." She could tell he was about to sob or something, and so she whispered something in his ear. Commander Mann's eyes flew open wide in astonishment.

"Something of a party this evening," he said, recovering from whatever Amelia had said to him. "Right, Commander Stewart?"

"A party is in order," Elizabeth said and laughed, "although I'm not sure I'm up to a major celebration."

The Space Colony, from hub to rim, was alive with the party spirit. Settlers actually lit bonfires in the Farm Zone. Everyone—at least an overflow crowd—met at Commander Stewart's for dinner.

✿ ✿ ✿

That evening, when most of the guests had gone, TF's father said, "We better do this, no? I'll never hear the end of it if we don't—from Colonel Smith, I mean."

Commander Mann cleared his throat. "We have a few items to attend to."

He lowered his voice. "Including an unauthorized journey to Phoebe, a breach of L5 Security, a violation of house arrest, unauthorized use of an MMU, and so on. Comments?"

"But those aren't actually the most interesting things," Amelia said. "We have an idea about Diana."

Commander Mann startled everybody by roaring with laughter, a deep belly laugh that Thor himself might have envied. "For you two, this is all in a mundane day's work, heh? Some of us are still fascinated by humdrum details. Shall we do a formal debriefing? I for one would like to know what the devil has been going on."

TF shrugged, straightened his shoulders, and spoke in his new-found baritone. He began at the beginning. "It's been a busy day. We were arrested."

"To not much effect, I understand," Commander Mann said to Amelia and TF.

"Well, it was dumb," Amelia said. "We were the only ones

who could figure out what was going on."

"You hardly gave us much of a chance," Commander Mann said. "We were working on it."

TF explained what had happened. Commander Mann mostly just nodded or shook his head, almost not believing. "Incredible," he said once.

When Amelia finished describing the actual landing on Phoebe, her chase through the asteroid, and breaking the computer code, Commander Mann coughed on his tea.

"Sorry," he said. "Went down the wrong tube."

"I'm sorry we disobeyed the rules," Amelia said. "I know the rules were there to protect us. You didn't want us out beyond the web because it was dangerous. But the whole Space Colony was in danger. The risk seemed worth it."

"I'm not sure children are capable of evaluating the risk involved," Commander Mann said.

"I don't know," Elizabeth said softly. "The children seem to have done a pretty fair job of evaluation and took appropriate—if not heroic, action—on a number of fronts. Living on frontiers has always forced children to grow up quickly. In this case the highest commendation this Colony has to bestow will immediately be entered into their files."

Her tone was such that she didn't need to add, "I so order it."

Later that evening, when the last sips of tea had been taken, Elizabeth looked at Amelia's father and nodded.

He stood up and said, "Among friends, I will admit it.

I will never again fail to take my daughter's advice."

There were chuckles all around. "What you don't know," he continued, "is what my wonderful daughter whispered into my ear earlier today. It was, 'Marry her, and do it fast.' Pursuant to this command, I have asked Commander Stewart to be my wife, and she has, to my great joy, accepted."

Amelia threw her arms around her father, pulling herself up out of her wheelchair. Then she sat back, wheeled around, and did the same thing to Elizabeth. For a moment, their hair overlapped, bright red and black.

✿　✿　✿

The next day, Amelia slept late, very late.

Then two calls came in over the communicator. The first was from Gran.

"Are you all right, Amelia? We've been watching the news. We were worried about you and about Jim. He looked so stressed. The whole thing was very, very scary."

Amelia went through the whole story again. When she was done, Gran just exhaled, as though she had been holding her breath.

"I'm just relieved," Gran said.

"Oh, Gran, it turned out very well."

"I have a little bit of news myself," Gran said. "Although not quite as earthshaking as yours. Gramps and I are leaving for the Space Station within the week. We weren't sure this was going to happen with all the activity up there. But the shore appears to be clear."

"You're coming here this week! Papa is getting married!"

"Goodness, we have hoots up the kazoo," Gran said and laughed.

"We'll have a big party," Amelia said. "I'll talk to Papa."

"Child, don't you need a rest?" Gran asked.

"No rest for the wicked," Amelia said. "And I have been very wicked lately."

The second call was almost more of a surprise. It was from Lila, the Space Cadet who had made fun of Amelia's overalls. Amelia answered her call coolly.

"Amelia, I…I wanted to talk to you," Lila faltered, not sounding at all like a robot, as she had when they had met before. "I owe you an apology."

Amelia did not respond. She didn't entirely trust the Space Cadets. Was this just another one of their little games? Lila continued, "You seemed strange, and you didn't seem to like us. Then you teamed up with that TF character."

"He's one of a kind," Amelia said. "It's hard for him to fit in. Me, too, for that matter."

"I hope all that can change," Lila said.

"How?" Amelia asked, with some suspicion.

"I was on TAS yesterday," Lila said. "Frankly, we were spying on you two. But when I heard you two playing that music, I just couldn't believe it! It was so beautiful. We don't have anything like that. What was it?"

"Beethoven," Amelia said. "We were playing a piano trio.

That means it has a violin, a cello, and a piano part. That was Piano Trio No. 1 in E-Flat, Opus One, Number One."

"I just know it was beautiful," Lila said. "It was hard to imagine that someone I knew could actually play music like that. Other Cadets heard it too. Some of us want to learn how to play an instrument."

Amelia was flabbergasted.

"Can you teach us?" Lila asked. "We would work very diligently."

"Favfav," Amelia said, grinning.

❅   ❅   ❅

There was quite a welcoming committee for Gramps and Gran when their ship finally docked at the hub.

Gramps looked a little frail after the ten-hour trip, but he was all smiles. His silver hair floated around his head like a halo. Gran flew about like a kid, exclaiming, "I have always wanted to fly, ever since I read *Peter Pan*.

After they had rested, Gramps and Gran were given the Farm Zone tour by Amelia and TF. "Today's the day we're releasing our terns," Amelia said. "They were a gift from Thor!"

The four of them walked along the same creek where Amelia had first met TF. They released the birds on the shore of the lake fed by the creek. The two birds scurried along the sand for a few yards. Then they wobbled into the air. After a short while, they took to swooping in long, smooth arcs.

❅   ❅   ❅

The wedding was held in Commander Stewart's home. Flowers and other plants were arranged in a huge bower. Gifts—jewelry, pottery, baskets, blankets—were brought from all over L5. Cheeses and bread and champagne were collected. Wood for the wedding fires was cut and split.

The day before the wedding, Thor and a band of Lunar Colonists arrived. As a gift, Thor brought an aquarium, stocked with brightly colored fish from a river in Africa. "These are jewels," he said. "Living jewels."

A delegation from the Federation of Nations on Earth also arrived for the event. Amelia suspected that Earth officials also wanted to make sure that hostilities had really been settled.

On the morning of the wedding, Commander Mann stood in Elizabeth's dining hall. "As part of this plan," he said to Amelia, "we will move from our quarters to share Elizabeth's home. How does that sit with you? You will have a real bed again."

He wrapped an arm around her shoulder.

Amelia answered, "There is nothing I'd like more. I think I will like having a mother again."

"I'm sure Elizabeth would love to have a daughter like you," Commander Mann said. "We've invited Gran and Gramps to stay with us for as long as they like. It would be nice to have the family in one place for a change, don't you think?"

"I think it would be marvelous."

Elizabeth swooped down on them. "Are we just about

ready?" she asked. She was dressed in a long white gown. Her black hair was braided down her back, and her eyes flashed with excitement.

"About Diana," Elizabeth said. "I have been giving her a lot of thought."

"That's my Commander Stewart for you," Commander Mann said and grinned. "On her wedding day, she wants to talk shop."

"Amelia and TF are right," Commander Stewart said. "Recommission the poor dear. Send her to Mars."

Commander Mann saluted, something Amelia had never seen her father do before.

Commander Stewart returned his salute, a slight smile tugging at the corners of her mouth.

Commander Mann continued, with a straight face, "I have already ordered a feasibility report, Sir. I knew if I didn't get right on it, the kids would arrange it all and probably go to Mars without us!"

Elizabeth looked at him with shining eyes and said, "Welcome back, Jim."

"I'm not supposed to be even talking to you, am I?" Commander Mann asked. "Aren't you supposed to be hidden away, giggling with your bridesmaids?"

"We do things differently nowadays on L5," Elizabeth said. "I'm certainly looking forward to dinner. I'm starving."

The ceremony began in the late afternoon, with the moon and the earth hanging on the horizon, through the heat and radiation shields. Even some of the Space Cadets appeared in their neat white uniforms but without their TAS earphones. Amelia was actually glad to see Lila. Several Space Cadets talked to TF about taking cello lessons from him, and he seemed pleased.

Thor, his red braid bright against his black tuxedo, performed the service, which was short, simple, and, Amelia thought, magnificent.

Then the couple kissed and it was over. Amelia cried, and she was not the only one. A grand old waltz filled the air. The happy couple danced all alone for a moment and then were slowly joined by others dancing in slow circles in the little space cleared among the crowd. Amelia watched from her wheelchair.

Suddenly, TF approached Amelia and bowed. "May I have this dance?" he asked, looking unexpectedly grown up in his suit. "Oh, TF!" Amelia protested.

"With a little help from your friend, of course." And TF picked her out of the chair as though she were a feather.

He turned with her slowly, a little awkwardly at first. She laughed out loud.

TF grinned too and swung her around. Amelia glanced up at the skyport, and saw that they were all dancing by the light of the moon as the Owl and the Pussycat had.

Steve Tracy was born in Albuquerque, New Mexico. He grew up on the coast of California and published his first story— in the *Monterey Peninsula Herald*—when he was in the fifth grade. He studied biology and English in college, where he also learned to scuba dive. He has taught chemistry labs at Indiana University and creative writing at Stanford University. When he was twenty-one he published his first story in the *New Yorker* and went on to win the Joseph Henry Jackson Award for fiction. Over the last twenty years, he has worked as a writer, a riding teacher, an editor of a paper, a reporter, a horseshoer and a cabinet maker. Today, he lives on a farm in California overlooking the Pacific Ocean with a cat and a rooster. Steve plays violin and tennis.